# DANGEROUS MEN

# DANGEROUS MEN

# GEOFFREY BECKER

*Winner of the* DRUE HEINZ LITERATURE PRIZE 1995

UNIVERSITY OF PITTSBURGH PRESS *Pittsburgh & London*

Published by the

University of Pittsburgh Press,

Pittsburgh, Pa. 15260

Copyright © 1995, Geoffrey Becker

Manufactured in the United States of America

Printed on acid-free paper

Library of Congress Cataloging-in-Publication Data

Becker, Geoffrey, 1959–

   Dangerous men / Geoffrey Becker.

     p.   cm.

   "Drue Heinz Literature Prize."

   ISBN 0-8229-3899-5 (cloth)

   I. Title.

PS3552.E2553D35   1995

813'.54—DC20     95-21964

          CIP

A CIP catalogue record for this book is available from the British Library.

Grateful acknowledgment is made to the following publications in which some of these
stories first appeared in slightly different form: *Crazyhorse* ("Magister Ludi"); *The
Crescent Review* ("Taxes"); *The Florida Review* ("Daddy D. and Short Time"); *Iowa
Journal of Literary Studies* ("Down at the Studio," formerly "Mighty Pup"); *Poet & Critic*
("El Diablo de La Cienega"); *Quarterly West* ("The Handstand Man"); *Sonora Review*
("Erin and Malcolm"); and *West Branch* ("Big Grey").

   "Bluestown" originally appeared in *The Chicago Tribune* and was reprinted in *The
North American Review*.

   The author would like to express his gratitude to the Copernicus Society of America
and James Michener for support during the writing of this book. Also, thanks to my close
friends and readers, Fred Leebron, Steve Rinehart, and especially Lynda Leidiger.

TO MY MOTHER AND FATHER

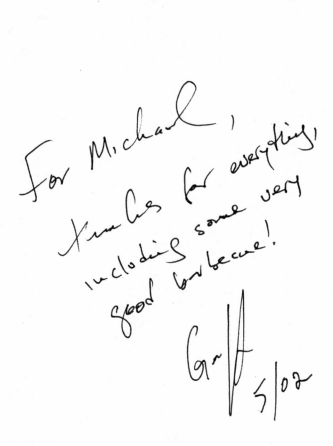

For Michael,
thanks for everything,
including some very
good barbecue!

Geoff 5/02

# CONTENTS

# DANGEROUS MEN

# DANGEROUS MEN

Calvin, a drummer from Long Island who lived down the hall from us, wore jeans and tight, white T-shirts, smoked Lucky Strikes, and had eyes that nervously avoided contact. He was nineteen and skinny, but in a muscular way that reminded me of a greyhound. It was the summer of 1974, and my friend Ed and I shared a dorm room in what had once been a cheap hotel, but was now part of the Berklee College of Music. One Saturday night, Calvin came to our room and laid out ten little purple pills.

"Eat 'em up, gentlemen," he said.

I looked over at Ed, who was laboring to get his hair into a rubber band. Ed hadn't had a haircut in three years, and from behind, since he was short, you'd swear he was a girl.

"What are they?" Ed asked.

"Magic beans," Calvin said, punching my arm. "I traded the old lady's cow for them."

I picked one up, then placed it carefully back down. A little color came off on my fingertips.

"UFO," he went on. "Got 'em off a sax player I met on the elevator. Cat worked with Buddy *Rich*." Calvin had a thing about Buddy Rich.

"So?"

I glanced over at my homework. I'd been trying to write out a horn arrangement for "Satin Doll." After nearly two hours' work, I was still on the third measure, and I was pretty sure my trumpet part had wandered below the instrument's range anyway. Lili Arnot, the girl I loved, smiled down happily from where I'd taped her photo above my desk, tanned and lovely against the unhealthy green of the cracked plaster wall.

They were more like little barrels than tablets. Ed and I each had two, Calvin six. I watched with amazement as he placed them one after another into his mouth. They tasted bitter, no matter how fast you got them down.

————

It was the kind of night where your skin itches and the heat seems to sweat the street life right out of the city's pores. I gave a drunk with an English accent fifty cents and he croaked his thanks, but I sensed it might be a mistake in the long run, because the other drunks glowered at me, memorizing my face. Calvin led us past a trio of sullen hookers and over to TK's, a bar across the street where we could get served. Ed and I were both underage.

We ordered a pitcher of Black Label and listened to him.

"Let me tell you guys something," Calvin said. "I am dying here. At home, I get laid four times a day, I'm serious."

Ed nodded. He had a steady girlfriend back in New Jersey, Deborah, whose sexual appetite was enormous. I'd convinced him to come with me to Boston and do this summer program, and though we didn't talk about it much, we both knew what he'd given up. What he might, in fact, have given up permanently, given Deborah's obvious and immediate needs.

"You guys want to see a picture of my girl?" Calvin pulled out his wallet and unfolded a piece of paper that looked suspiciously as if it had been cut from a magazine. Ed looked at it first, then handed it to me.

"Nice," I said. It was a photo of a redhead, kneeling on a hand-woven carpet, wearing an Indian headband and nothing else. I had to admit, if you were going to pick a girl to have delusions about, this was the one. Her eyes looked right out at you from the picture, not in a cheap way, or even a sexy one. It was more like she was studying you, as if she were seriously interested in who this person holding her in the flat of his hand might be.

When Calvin went to the bathroom, I asked Ed what he thought.

"I think that is one fucked-up individual, is what I think."

"He ate six," I said.

"We think he ate them. How can we be sure?"

"You think he tricked us?" The pills had begun to kick in, and whatever they were, they were cut with speed. I could feel myself tensing up. "Why would he trick us?"

"I don't know, man. The guy falls in love with magazine pictures."

"Maybe we're just paranoid."

"We're definitely paranoid. That doesn't mean we're wrong. Sometimes it's *smart* to be paranoid."

"We could just go," I said. "Go see a movie or something. He'd probably be OK by himself."

Ed stroked his chin. He'd taken his hair down again, and already he was turning into something gnomelike and medieval, a strangely proportioned face peering out from behind curtains. "The thing is, if he really did take six, we can't leave him alone. It wouldn't be right. Look at us. Now multiply this by three. Plus, the dude's a couple eggs short of a dozen as it is."

"Right," I said. "What do we do with him?"

"I don't know," said Ed. "Have some fun. Go out. What do we usually do?"

———

We drank another pitcher, then headed out into the evening. Ed and I wanted to see Andy Warhol's *Frankenstein*, which was rated X and in 3-D. Calvin told us he had something else in mind.

"There's this park not far away," he said. "Fags go there. I heard about it from one of the kitchen staff. They go and hang around in the bushes until some other fag comes along and then pair off."

This was a new concept to me. I knew there were homosexuals in the world, but I hadn't imagined them lurking about in bushes at night like zombies.

"What do you say we go kick some faggot butt?" asked Calvin.

We were standing in the shadow of a tall building smoking cigarettes, buzzing with the UFO, though some of that edge had been taken off nicely by the beer. It was cooler than it had been all day and my energy was high. I made a gallant attempt to run straight up the side of the building, but only ended up landing a good kick to the stone.

"Yeah," said Ed. "That sounds good."

I'd never really been in any fights, and I didn't know how I'd react. I'd never met a faggot, at least not to my knowledge, though there were some guys at school we had our doubts about. Beating them up had never crossed my mind. But Ed and Calvin seemed to have bonded on the issue. I figured I could just go along, see what happened.

We wandered through streets that seemed mirror images of themselves, angled and dark, the tall, brown faces of the row houses looking out at us with the calmness of age and location. The pavement was swollen and soft and the metal of the closely parked cars ticked with the day's heat. Stopping to admire a GTO, Calvin asked us which we'd rather have, a Goat or a T-bird, and when Ed said T-bird, Calvin told him he was full of shit.

"Goats *go*," he said, as if the sound of the words were themselves somehow proof.

For a while, I forgot about our purpose and tried to organize the arrhythmic thops of Ed's and Calvin's boots against the stone slabs of the sidewalk while I floated along behind, silent as a balloon. I could still see the blank staves of my music tablet, and now various rhythmic figures deported themselves for me, grouping and re-grouping like children at a dance recital. Rhythm was my big weakness; I just couldn't translate what I heard to paper. That spring, I'd found a book in my parents' bedroom about people who'd made miraculous breakthroughs on LSD — an electrical en-gineer who'd suddenly understood how to solve a problem he'd been working on for ten years, a schizophrenic who'd managed to rid herself of the voices that had plagued her all her life — and now I wondered if I couldn't make a similar leap. As we walked, I ex-perimented by plugging in time signatures: 4/4, 9/8, 5/8. With each change the dots would all shift. Though I doubted the ac-curacy of what I was seeing, I was definitely seeing something, and I was proud of my brain for being able to conjure answers so quickly, right or wrong. The more I thought about it, though, the more artificial the whole idea seemed. The world didn't divide up neatly, it fragmented in strange and unusual ways. It was only our need to make sense of it that made us believe in things like time signatures, or minutes and hours for that matter. Or days of the week, cities, states. Even countries.

We'd stopped moving and were waiting to cross a street. "The problem is limits," I said.

Calvin looked hard at me. "The problem is faggots."

Embarrassed, I bummed a cigarette from Ed, who was smoking Kools that summer, tearing the packs open at the bottom corner the way the black kids at our school did. I thought it was pretty affected, but I hadn't said anything to him about it. I was hoping he'd come around on his own.

"So where is this park?" It seemed to have grown a lot darker out. I didn't think I was having fun.

Calvin's face puckered with irritation. "Don't worry about it. We're close."

It occurred to me that probably, there was no park. There were no faggots. These things were as imaginary as the girl in his wallet.

In the distance, the CITGO sign hung in the air like a single, luminous eye, opening and closing with reptilian removal. Also there was, quite suddenly, music.

"We're near the water," said Ed.

———

On the grass by the Hatch shell, a festival was in progress. People beat on drums and blew saxophones and danced. Someone was shooting off medium-sized fireworks, and every few minutes there would be a whoosh followed by an explosion overhead, as red, green, silver, and gold flowers bloomed in the night sky. A woman with her face painted white wearing a clown wig and a Mr. Donut apron hurled handfuls of miniature glazed donuts up into the air. I asked her what was going on.

"You don't know?"

"No, I don't."

"The president resigned," she said.

"Who?"

"*Nixon!* Isn't it great?" She gave me a couple of donuts and I returned to my friends. Ed was doing push-ups, while Calvin tossed a small knife in the air, catching it each time by the blade end.

"It's Nixon," I reported. "He resigned."

Ed got to his feet, grinning, and slapped me five. It was like our team had won the Superbowl. I hadn't followed the specifics carefully, but I had watched with fascination the haggard images of the man that had appeared on TV over the past few months. There was no doubt in my mind the president had lost it, had become Humphrey Bogart in *The Caine Mutiny*, hollow eyed, intent on discovering who'd eaten his strawberries. I had only the vaguest memories of the Kennedy assassination. I'd been in summer camp for the moon landing, 150 of us squinting at one snowy TV screen that had been set up in the dining hall. Here was something I'd remember.

"Are you guys with me, or what?" Calvin asked. He didn't even look at the knife, just flipped it. He never missed, but even so, I kept thinking at any moment he was liable to lose a finger or two.

"What about the movie?" I suggested. In the flickering riverlight, Calvin had become something of an old newsreel himself.

"Movie?" He toed the earth, kicking a small hunk of dirt to the side. "I want to kick some *ass*."

"You don't know where they are," I reminded him. "What have we been doing for the last hour?"

"I know where they are."

"Here," I said, distributing the donuts. Ed popped his in his mouth whole. Calvin slit his into pieces with his knife, dropping the sections to the ground.

"So, where are they?" I asked.

"What are you saying?"

I told him I wasn't saying anything. His eyes, I thought, had a peculiarly dead look to them, as if they'd been replaced with lug nuts.

"You think I'm shitting you? You think they aren't out there? This whole town is crawling with faggots." He looked around, as if some might be listening at this very moment.

"But *where?*" I asked. "This is all I want to know. Where are we going? You say we're going somewhere, and then we walk and walk, and we don't get there."

Calvin scratched at the side of his nose with his middle finger. He'd begun to glow a little, like something irradiated.

"Forget it," he said. "I don't need you guys. I'll do this alone."

"Hey," said Ed. "We're coming."

———

We hadn't gone far when I saw that Ed was holding something. Calvin walked a few paces ahead of us, leading us back into the city, away from the water. It was a kitten.

"Where'd she come from?" I asked.

"In the park," he said. "I'm naming her Ella."

"What if she belongs to someone?"

"She belongs to me. She's a stray."

"But how do you *know* that? Maybe someone was just out playing with their kitten and she wandered off. Maybe they're out looking for her right now."

"Relax, man," said Ed. "You worry too much."

"I'm just saying it might not be a stray."

"It might not be a cat, either. They look like kittens, so we take them into our homes, then they tear us open while we're asleep, climb inside, and assume our bodies."

"All right, all right," I said. "But she's going to be your responsibility. Don't expect your father and me to feed her and change her litter box."

There was a screech of brakes up ahead, followed by a kind of thump sound, and I saw Calvin get tossed a few feet into the air backward, then fall hard to the ground. Ed and I ran to him. He was just lying there on his side. The guy driving the car was already out and on his knees.

"He walked right out in front of me," the guy said. "I think I killed him. Oh, lord, I think he's dead."

I knew he wasn't dead because I could see him breathing. "Calvin," I said. "Are you all right?" There was no answer.

"We ought to get the cops," said Ed.

"Maybe we could bypass that," said the man, uneasily. "I mean, I don't see that the cops are necessary here. Why don't we just get an ambulance?"

"Yeah," I said, remembering the hash pipe tucked in my pocket. "Let's bypass the cops."

"Out of nowhere," the guy was saying. He was older, a black guy, dressed in a suit, and while I was worried about Calvin, I felt bad for him, too. His car was a Cadillac, a new one. He'd just been minding his business, trying to get someplace. He didn't deserve us.

Ed helped Calvin to a sitting position. His eyes were open and he seemed to be able to see. "You blew it big time," he said to the guy. "My dad's a lawyer. I intend to own that car of yours."

"Don't mind him," said Ed. "He's not right in the head."

"Can you breathe?" I asked. "Can you move everything?"

"Well, I guess I'll be getting along," said the driver.

"Don't let him go anywhere," Calvin directed us. "Hold him."

For a tense second or two, Ed and I looked at each other, waiting to see what the other would do. I didn't feel like grabbing anyone, though I wasn't sure about Ed. I sensed there might actually be a part of him that wanted to beat up strangers. The man edged away from us, got into his car and pulled away in a squealing of tires.

"Pussies," said Calvin.

"You're all right," I said after we'd all been silent for a little while. "Come on and let's head back to the dorm."

I tried to help him to his feet, but he shook off my hand and got up on his own. His jeans were torn down the side of one leg where he'd slid on the asphalt, and his arm was pretty scraped up, too. He brushed himself off and spat a couple of times.

"Amazing," said Ed. "You could be dead right now. You probably should be. What happened?"

"I don't know," he said. "I don't remember that much about it." His hands shook uncontrollably as he attempted to light a cigarette. After five matches, he got it going. "Where'd the cat come from?"

Ed put Ella up on his shoulder. "I found her."

Calvin took his cigarette and drew circles in the air in front of the kitten, who was fascinated. The orange ember left visible trails, like pinwheels in the dark.

———

The skinny, acned night desk guy was playing chess by himself and didn't even look up as we came in. The elevator stopped more or less at the fifth floor and we jumped down into the hallway, except for Calvin, who'd been limping slightly. He sat, dangled his legs, then stood. Outside our door we stopped as I hunted for the key. I was hoping Calvin would keep on going — I'd had enough of him for one night.

"What are you guys going to do?" he asked.

"I'm kind of tired," I lied. I felt as if I'd probably be awake for the next week. This was not a happy, fun drug we'd taken. This was a twist-your-head-up-in-knots drug. I just wanted it to be over.

"Mind if I hang? I don't like it when that guy goes off."

For the past week or so, right around midnight, someone on one of the upper floors had been letting loose with a series of bloodcurdling screams. We called him the Wildman. Legends had begun to appear scrawled in marker on the elevator wall: "Wildman Lives" and "Have you made your Peace?" While we all figured it was just some student with a twisted sense of humor and probably not the Angel of Death, the screams themselves were definitely unnerving.

I was a little surprised. "You're not scared, are you?"

"I just don't like it." Behind him, the dim hallway gaped like a mouth. He was vibrating slightly, possibly out of fear, but it could have been leftover nerves from the accident, or even just a trick of the hall light.

We let him in. Ed mashed up some saltines with water for Ella and put them in a dish. Calvin sat on the floor and took off his shoe. His ankle was swollen up like a grapefruit and had begun to turn a greenish purple.

"You walked on that?" Ed asked.

"I didn't know what it looked like."

"But you must have felt something," I said. "I mean, Jesus, that's ugly."

"I felt something, I guess. I don't know."

It was a bad moment. I thought he might cry. He kept staring at his ankle and shaking his head. "We should ice it," I said. Someone needed to take charge here.

"Where do we get ice at this time of night?" said Ed. He brought over our bottle of Jim Beam and some plastic cups.

I took the elevator back down to the Pepsi machine, pumped it with all our laundry quarters, got back on with an armful of cold cans.

Between the third and fourth floors, the elevator stalled. Then the lights flickered and went out. I stood there in total darkness holding five cans of soda, feeling their icy outlines against my ribs. From someplace high above, a person began to scream, making the kind of sounds that might come from someone being turned on a rack, or having their skin slowly peeled from them. I bent my knees and lowered myself to the floor. I decided to separate myself from this. Filtered through the elevator shaft, the sounds had a surreal quality, and I tried to imagine how one might notate them. After a while, I couldn't even tell if my eyes were open or not. I dropped the sodas and put my hands over my ears.

The howling stopped about a minute before the power kicked back in and the light returned. I collected the cans, stood and pushed the button for our floor again, taking comfort in the familiar graffiti, the fake wood-grain control panel, the ordinariness of it all.

———

Calvin sat with his foot up on Ed's bed. I arranged the Pepsis around his ankle.

"How's that feel?" I asked.

"Cold."

The pale blotchiness of Calvin's cheeks made me think of packaged supermarket tomatoes.

"Whoever that guy is," said Ed, "he's seriously whacked."

"Vietnam," said Calvin. "You know that guy with the blonde hair and beard who always eats by himself, wears an Army jacket?" He sipped at his drink, put it down hard on the edge of the desk. "He was over there. Went out on patrol with a buddy, and his buddy tripped a mine. Blew off part of his leg. That guy dragged a man two miles through the jungle, a guy who was already dead. When he found out, something in him just sort of snapped."

I knew for a fact this wasn't true. The guy with the beard who ate by himself was from Spokane, Washington, where he taught second grade and played piano at a Holiday Inn lounge, evenings. I'd talked to him once, when we'd both been waiting for the elevator. His name was Pat, and the main thing about him was his shyness. Of course, he might still have been the Wildman, but if so, it had nothing to do with Vietnam, or legs getting blown off.

"Where do you get your information?" I asked.

He shook his head. "Classified. I could tell you, but then I'd have to shoot you."

Ed coughed.

"You are so amazingly full of shit. I've talked to that guy. He's never been out of the country."

"Do you believe everything people tell you?"

"Do you believe everything that pops into your head?"

I looked over at Ella, who'd found herself a spot on Ed's bed, where she was busily licking one extended leg. The radio, which had been playing jazz, segued into crunching guitars. The water stain on our wall reminded me of something from biology class. I took one of the cans from next to Calvin's leg, tore off its pop-top.

He was silent, looking around the room. His eyes rested on my picture of Lili Arnot. "That your woman?"

I nodded. In truth, Lili Arnot would have probably been surprised to know I even *had* a picture of her, let alone that I was telling people she was my "woman." In the picture, she wore cut-offs and a white blouse and held a tennis racket under one arm.

"She gave me a blowjob once."

His face was a marionette's, grinning, wooden, vaguely evil. I hurled my open soda at it. The can glanced off the side of his head, continuing on to the wall, then to the floor where it spurted and frothed for a few seconds onto the stained carpet.

Considering his ankle, Calvin came at me with amazing speed. He threw me against the opposite wall. I'd cut him with the can, and blood dripped down over his ear. There was an oniony smell of perspiration about him, mixed with a sweeter scent of hair stuff. I put my hands around his neck and tried to choke him, while at the same time, he threw hard punches at my stomach and sides. There was a kind of purity to the moment, as when a thick August afternoon finally transforms itself into rain. This was where we'd been heading tonight, after all. If we couldn't beat up fags, we could at least beat up each other. I figured he might kill me, but I refused to worry. That was my role — the guy who worried — and I was tired of it. Ed shouted at us to stop, but we'd locked up like jammed gears. Calvin bit my shoulder and I jerked forward with all my weight, enough to push him off balance, causing him to step back. He cursed loudly and sat on the bed, where he pounded his fist up and down on the mattress.

"What?" I said. "What happened?"

"He twisted it worse," said Ed, going over to take a look. "Maybe it's broken."

"Fuck, fuck, fuck, fuck, fuck," said Calvin.

"You want to go to the hospital?"

"We can't take him to the hospital," said Ed. "They'll take one look at him and call the cops. Look at his pupils. They're the size of dimes."

"I'm all right," said Calvin, grimacing.

We decided on more aspirin and repacked the sodas around his foot.

No one said anything for a while. My sides hurt where I'd been punched, but basically I was OK, though I did feel a little stupid. Ed, who was wearing his "Bird Lives" T-shirt, started doing curls with a thirty-pound barbell. Calvin reached over and took my notebook along with a pair of number-two pencils off the desk, began playing drums atop my arranging homework. I didn't stop him, I just watched, painfully aware of my inadequate pencil marks on the stiff paper. They looked like a road construction project abandoned after only a few feet. Finally, I asked, "Did the lights go off here?"

"Lights?" said Calvin. "What lights?"

"When I was on the elevator, the lights died."

"Somebody should put that elevator out of its misery."

I sat down in a chair and had one of Ed's Kools. There were less than two weeks left to the summer. Soon, other people would have this room. It was wrong to think that our presence would linger on, though it was to this notion that I realized I'd been grasping all along, the idea that in some way we were etching ourselves onto the air, leaving shadows that would remain forever.

After a minute, Calvin put aside the pencils, took his knife out again and began flipping it. He seemed to have forgotten all about our fight, or the way we'd let him down earlier. He seemed to have forgotten about everything. I thought about the rockets we'd watched by the water, the way they rose in one big fiery line, then separated into smaller projectiles, burning out slowly in their own, solo descent.

"I know these two girls that share an apartment a few blocks from here," he said. "I met them at a record store. Very cool, very good-looking, and their parents are away. I'm serious — we could go over there."

"All three of us?" I said.

"Yes, all three of us." He was suddenly enthusiastic. "They wouldn't mind. We could say we were hungry, get them to make us eggs. That would get us in, then we could just see what happened from there."

"I am a little hungry," Ed admitted.

"You really want to go out again?" I asked. "You've been through a lot. Think about it. You got hit by a car."

He wasn't listening. "The hard part will be getting past the security guy at their building. We'll need a diversion. After that, we're home free." He dug a piece of paper from his wallet, and on it there was indeed a name, Nicole, written in loopy, high-school-girl handwriting. It was followed by an address. There was a distinct possibility that this was real.

"We'll get 'em to make us omelets," he said.

For a moment, I saw Calvin as a distillation of my own, ugly soul, and in his grinning, wicked eyes I thought I saw a reflection of all the bad things I'd done, as well as the ones I would do.

"It's really pretty late," I said, quietly.

But Calvin was already putting on his shoes.

# DARLING NIKKI

I'm soft and always have been. Nikki's the tough one, the one who always got into fights, who couldn't wear a pair of pants two days without ripping the knees out climbing something. Which was kind of a gyp, because when I got old enough to want them, there was nothing for me to inherit — no lipstick or mascara, no pretty clothes she'd grown out of. Mama had to start fresh with me on everything, and what with Mr. Quitts doing most of the providing for us, I couldn't just stick out my hand and ask for, say, money for a bottle of Rive Gauche. Not that I was deprived or anything; I had plenty of nice stuff, and I hate people that complain about how awful it was for them as kids and how if only this, or if only that, and everything would have been different.

It was me that convinced Nikki about nursing school, after that idiot coach at St. Mary's switched her from first base to outfield, then forced her to start throwing differently. You don't take the best first baseman in the state of Iowa and put her in right field—it's borderline criminal. Nikki said it was like buying a Harley, then taking it apart to build a go-cart. The amount of muscle damage she did to herself, you'd almost think she was trying to prove the point.

After she was out of the hospital and done sulking, I showed her some of my catalogues. She paged through them for a little while, stopping at the end where there was this picture of a smiling graduate, wearing her RN uniform, holding two little children, one black and one white, by the hand.

"Karina?" she asked me, curling the corner of the page. "Do you think I can do this?"

"Sure," I told her. "It's not hard. A little chemistry, some biology, five clinical semesters, and we'll have our BSN's."

"Not hard for you." Her face tightened up and I knew what she was thinking. I was always going to be a nurse—I'd been telling people about it since I was five. Lord knows where I got the idea, it just got planted there, somehow. But Nikki's talent was softball. The best grade she'd ever gotten in school was a B once, in a social studies class where she did a report on motorcycle gangs. This was a real change in plans.

"I'll help you," I said. I meant it, too. I loved my sister, and there hadn't been many moments in life where I'd seen her vulnerable. I also knew her, and I knew that if she decided she was going to do something, she'd do it with fire and determination. She's a mule about things if she wants to be. Just look at her shoulder.

Nikki drove us up to Iowa City on her bike, and it was kind of interesting, because I'm sure people watching us zip by thought she was a guy and I was her girlfriend. I had on a skirt that showed a lot of leg, and Nikki had just cut her hair almost totally off. It was a hot day, and I could imagine what she felt like under that leather vest, but she's a stickler about how she looks when she's on her bike. Leather is essential. Me, I was glad for the breeze.

We found an apartment in a new building, with carpeting that went right into the bathroom and a refrigerator that Nikki immediately stocked with a twelve-pack. Mr. Quitts had given us each a hundred dollars as we were leaving, and he couldn't have surprised us more if he'd told us he were coming along too. Not that he's an ungenerous person — he's provided well for Mama nearly ten years now, and never really had a harsh word for either of us, except for the time Nikki borrowed his truck without asking and ran it out of gas. But pouring concrete for a living, day after day, has in my opinion sort of crusted over his soul. We had his money in our wallets, but it was hard to say if it had been a gift, or a loan, or what, and neither of us felt exactly right about spending it.

The manager, Lou, gave us our keys and showed us where he lived, which was two units over, in a smaller apartment, on the ground level. Or rather, subground — his living-room window looked out on a sunken concrete deck where he had one plastic chair and a slightly old-looking bowl of cat food.

"Any problems, you call me," he said. "I'm here most of the time, except when I'm in class. If I'm not, there's a machine." Lou was dark, with short, thick hair, and arms that pushed out of the sleeves of his polo shirt like carved table legs.

I asked him what he was studying and he told us dentistry. "I have one year to go, then I'm going to move to Colorado and get into a general practice. I figure two years of that, max, then I go out on my own. You girls have very nice teeth." He looked back and forth from my mouth to Nikki's and I pressed my lips together, because it was like having someone try to look down your shirt. "Is that a cap?" he asked.

Nikki reached up and touched it with her forefinger, while I rolled my eyes and for a second almost forgot who'd done it to her, which was me, when I was thirteen and she was trying to teach me to throw. Mama called from the house to say she'd made us some sandwiches, and Nikki turned to answer just as I let go of the ball. Being bad at sports doesn't always mean being a poor aim. It can also mean being generally out of sync with what's going on. I knocked Nikki over like a bowling pin — she wasn't expecting it. The tooth cracked right in half. The amazing thing is, she never blamed me. She always says she should have seen it coming.

"It's yellowing a little," said Lou. "I could fix that."

"I like my tooth," she said. "I'm used to it."

Lou stepped closer to her, seeming to think about this. He had the outline of an enormous wallet protruding from the back pocket of his jeans. "You know," he said, "you're right. That tooth is you — it's part of your personality." As if, after twenty minutes, he could really know the first thing about her personality.

"Jeez," I said to Nikki when he was gone. "What a charming guy. My respect for dentists just dropped about eighty points."

She was standing at the window, looking out into the street. Her new haircut jutted toward the ceiling like the crest of some bird. "Maybe we should have a party," she said. "A kind of housewarming."

"We don't know anybody," I pointed out. "Except Lou, of course."

She turned, looked at me, shrugged and went into the kitchen for a beer. Right then, I knew we were headed for trouble — everything seemed to shout it to me, the blank walls of the apartment, the little red fibers in the otherwise blue carpeting. Nikki's Harley stood out by the curb, sunlight reflecting off one of the mirrors. We could just get back on and leave, I thought. Maybe we should.

Nikki knew about as much about men as she did about higher math. She'd drunk plenty of beers with them, even made out a couple of times at parties back in high school. But basically they were a mystery to her. Sometimes, when I used to talk to the Gray brothers on the phone, she'd come into my room, sit in the wicker chair next to my collection of plastic horses, and just listen. I didn't mind. Troy Gray was Nikki's age and I dated him for over a year, but all that while I was secretly seeing his brother Graham, too. The fact was, I liked them both, and they made me feel like somebody, like a queen. Nikki couldn't believe I'd kept it up so long, without either of the brothers finding out about the other. "Harlot," she'd say after I hung up. Then she'd tackle me and we'd wrestle and try to tickle each other until I gave in, which I always did.

———

I didn't care for Lou much, and it about killed me to see Nikki mooning over him. It just didn't fit her. She kept coming up with excuses to go down to his apartment and borrow a hammer, or a wrench or something, and often she let his cat, Yowzer, come in to our place, even though I'm allergic. Yowzer was a slender thing, with a checkerboard face — black in two quarters, white in the others. He had scars all over him from fighting with the other local cats, and I didn't like the way he looked at me. Lou was always forgetting to leave a window open for him, so we got to see a fair bit of Yowzer.

I decided something had to be done, so at our party, I made a fool of myself over Lou. Well, not exactly — I didn't hover over him or anything like that. Nikki did the hovering. I just went out of my way to talk to every guy there, always in sight of Lou. Most were friends of his, though we had a few neighbors over, too. Men have no faith in their own judgment when it comes to women — they'll always wait to see what their friends think, and then that's what they think too. It's pathetic, really, but predictable as winter. If Mel Gibson started dating fat women, I bet half the men in the country would begin hanging around outside Weight Watchers.

My goal was protection. Lou was not for Nikki, but by the time she got around to figuring that out on her own, her classes would be down the tubes, along with this whole nursing business. School didn't even start for another three days, but since it was my idea, I felt some obligation to keep her on track. At the same time, I have to admit, working on Lou was kind of fun, too, if you call shooting a big, conceited fish in a barrel fun.

About two A.M., things had dwindled down to just me, Nikki, Lou, and a friend of his named Forrest or Tree, something like that — he'd introduced himself to me hours ago and I'd promptly forgotten, and it seemed too late to ask now. Apparently, it didn't matter, because he answered to Weasel, or just plain Weez, and that fit him better anyway. Weez wanted to go up to the reservoir in Coralville for a swim.

"I'm up for it," said Nikki. She looked at me. I shrugged.

"Weez, you got your truck here?" asked Lou. He had on white jeans (very tight in the butt) and a tank top and a big, silvery wristwatch. Someday, he was going to have that big wallet of his stuffed with money, and he was well aware of it — it gave him a kind of easy confidence.

"The back's full of lumber," said Weez, "and we can't all fit up front."

"Lou can ride with me," said Nikki. "You guys meet us up there."

I smiled and ran a mental checklist of self-defense tactics for possible use in the cab of Weez's truck. Then I made significant eye contact with Lou, which did not go unnoticed by Nikki. "Sure," I said. "We'll see you there."

They went out first because I wanted to straighten up a little, and Weez needed the bathroom. In my bedroom, I quick-changed into a swimsuit. I watched out the window in amazement as Nikki started up the bike, then got back off and let Lou take the front position. Nikki slipped on behind him and put her arms around his waist. It was a first. I don't think anyone had ever driven Nikki's bike.

"Ready?" asked Weez, coming back into the room. He wasn't as ugly as his name — he even looked like a person you could get to like in a freckly, redheaded sort of way, if he'd had a few less beers.

"One condition," I told him. "I drive."

---

They were already there, sitting together on the sand, passing a bottle of peppermint schnapps. The moonlight silvered the reservoir, and its gentle, rocking sound was inviting — like a full tub just after you've turned off the water.

Nikki stripped off her clothes to go in, and I could see Weez and Lou staring, though trying to look like they weren't. Nikki's body is a little squat, but it's also really nice to look at, even with the scar from her operation. Solid. With her just getting naked and diving in, I felt a little silly in my Speedo, but I was grateful for it all the same. When Lou took off his clothes, I decided he must not be working that hard in dental school, since it was obvious he spent all his time at the gym. He dove in after Nikki, and the two of them splashed off into the night like a mermaid pursued by a sailor.

Before Weez and I could even think about following, there were two cops with flashlights waving us over. They shouted out at Nikki and Lou to come back, and while we waited, they checked my and Weez's IDs. When they finally came back to shore, one of the cops ran his light right over Nikki, very slowly. He told us we were not allowed here this hour of night, and that skinny-dipping was never allowed, and all the time he kept the light on her. I think we were all embarrassed, except for Nikki. She seemed more mad about the interruption than anything else. She stood there glaring at him, even after he finally clicked off the light, leaving her just a grayish moon-ghost like the rest of us.

———

Before we went to bed that night, we made a deal. "Look, I guess I ought to tell you," she said. "I'm kind of interested in Lou." Yowzer, locked out of Lou's again, ran through her legs and hopped up onto the arm of our living-room chair.

"Well, stop the presses."

"And I think he likes me, too."

"Sister, he's a man. Of course he likes you — he wants to jump your bones. After what you showed him tonight, he probably thinks he can."

"I saw how you were looking at him, and I saw how he looked back."

"That's my point."

She scratched Yowzer between the ears and the cat responded by rolling onto its side, and falling backward onto the cushion of the chair. "I just want you to stay out of it."

"All right, then," I said. "But I want you to promise me that you'll put schoolwork ahead of everything else, including Lou. You need to establish priorities. I'm not attracted to Lou at all. I'm just afraid for you — I want this to work for us both."

She smiled. "I knew we could straighten this out. I'd hate to have to compete with you, Kare. You're too damn cute."

I could feel myself flush. It took a lot for her to say that, I knew.

"I wouldn't want to compete with you, either," I said.

———

School was hard on Nikki. We went to all our classes together, spent evenings in the library going over problems for chemistry, memorizing terms for psych. Sometimes she'd get frustrated and storm out of the house, get on her motorcycle and take off for parts unknown, cranking the engine so high it practically screamed. But it seemed to work—she'd come back relaxed, calm, and ready to begin again. I was proud.

It had been over a month since the night at the reservoir and it seemed to me that things had gotten normal enough. Nikki was at the gym running when Lou came by the apartment, looking for Yowzer. I told him I hadn't seen him.

"He's been missing for a whole day," Lou said. "I'm a little worried."

"Did you call the animal shelter?"

"Yeah," he said. "Nothing. Hey, I was thinking about going out for Chinese food. Would you like to come?"

I'd already eaten, but it was just some frozen stuff. I was prepared on all my classes. "We can't let Nikki know," I said. "She'd be furious. It takes her a lot longer to study than me, and I don't want to rub it in."

———

At the restaurant he talked on and on about the people in his class—who was going to be successful and who wasn't, where the best markets were for a new dentist, the advantages and disadvantages of different types of practices. Every now and then, to emphasize a point, he'd reach over and touch my hand, and each time, I'd withdraw it. But somehow, the last time he did it, I didn't, and his settled gently over mine like a thick, warm glove.

"What do you think?" he asked.

I realized that I had not followed anything he'd said for the last few minutes, and I tried vainly to retrieve something from the air. "About what?"

"The Mercedes versus the Jaguar."

My opinions on cars were solely the result of listening to Nikki, and I thought how it should have been her, not me, having this conversation. "German cars are a little clunky."

He grinned. "Exactly what I think. Efficient and solid, but no spirit. It's why they lost the war."

I felt suddenly guilty. I had betrayed Nikki, in a way, just by coming here with him, even if, as I knew for a fact, he had no chance at all with me. All right, he was kind of cute, but he was also a jerk — just look at the way he treated his cat. I tried to take back my hand, but he held on, fixing me with those big, dark eyes of his.

"We have to go," I said. "I'm sorry."

———

I should have just gone home, but I let Lou talk me into stopping over for a nightcap, and then there was this uncomfortable moment when he kissed me and I couldn't decide what to do exactly. I didn't want the kiss, but on the other hand, I didn't want to hurt his feelings, so I kissed back and we sort of hugged each other and rocked back and forth in the middle of his living room to an old Steely Dan album.

We'd both had a good bit to drink at the restaurant, followed by some of this cinnamon schnapps he had, but I really wasn't prepared for what happened next, which was that he lifted me right up off my feet, just scooped me into the air like in some forties musical. Three seconds later, I was floating on his water bed and he was over me, nuzzling my neck. He was like a fire I'd poured kerosene on. I thought, Oh, so this is how it happens. And then I thought, Well, I did give him the impression, after all. Meanwhile, he was grinding away above me like a cement mixer.

"You're crushing me," I said. "Really."

"You are so sexy," he mumbled. I realized that clothes were coming off, in particular, mine. "Hey," I said. "Hey, hey. Whoa there." I was suddenly scared. Lou's body felt like it was made of steel and hard rubber, and it wasn't going away.

From where we were, we couldn't hear Nikki. Probably, she'd knocked a time or two. The door was open anyway, so she just walked in. When she came into the bedroom and figured out what was happening, she was on Lou in a second, bringing his arm up behind his back in a position that could have easily broken it. At the same time, she bit his ear right through.

He howled. I slid out from under him and got to my feet, shaking, vaguely afraid she might come after me next. She held

Lou down a bit longer and I felt completely miserable, because this was the guy she'd been lusting after ever since we got to town, and now I'd ruined things permanently. There was blood all over my neck from Lou's ear, and when Nikki let him up, I could see some on her mouth, too, which wasn't real attractive.

"Your cat's upstairs," she said. Both Lou and I stared at her. Nikki had on a short black skirt, heels, and a white cotton top open to the third button.

"Come on, Kare." She took my hand and led me out of there.

———

Back in our apartment, Yowzer was on the kitchen counter working on a bowl of milk.

"Look, Nikki . . . " I said, but she interrupted me.

"Would you do me a favor?"

"Sure."

"Redo this makeup?"

It was after midnight, and we certainly weren't about to go anywhere.

She had a little smear of Lou's blood dried on her chin that made her look like a kid who'd been eating chocolate cake and getting it all over. Looking closely, I could see what she meant — she'd used a foundation that was far too dark for her, then put a healthy application of rouge over that. She'd skipped her eyes entirely. The effect was odd — like someone interrupted in the middle of getting ready for a night at the opera.

In the bathroom, we used cold cream, then washed and dried her face, first with a complexion soap, afterward with some witch hazel. I applied a lighter foundation. We're both pretty pale skinned, though I tend to get blotchier. Nikki's skin color is nice and consistent, and it's amazingly soft to the touch, much softer than mine.

"Close your eyes," I said.

She looked at me suspiciously. "What for?"

"Liner." I held it up.

Her lids flickered as I ran a delicate stroke just at the tip, not so much as to be really obvious, but enough to draw attention to the eyes, make them seem bigger. Then I put on a little mascara to fill out and lengthen her lashes. I gave her a hint of rouge, working it in with my fingertips in gentle circles. I put a bit of powder on her nose to get rid of the shine.

"We just need to decide on a lipstick," I said. "I've got about twenty to choose from. You could even go black if you want to be really outrageous."

She looked at me oddly. "I want to look pretty, not like an old banana."

I showed her my lineup. "I've got this new stuff, 'Lasting Kiss,' that's supposed to hold up for days. I haven't tried it yet, but you can eat with it on, sleep with it, work out, go swimming."

"That's perfect," she said. "Something that will last."

I put it on her, then put some styling gel in her hair and fussed with it for a while, though it was still so short that there weren't a lot of options. When I was finished she stood and turned to see herself in the mirror on the door.

"Oh, man," she said.

"Wait." As a final touch, I put a dab of Rive Gauche behind each of her ears. " 'Darling Nikki,' " I said. We used to play that Prince song all the time, back at the house, before she went off to St. Mary's. I put my arm around her.

She really did look beautiful, and I suddenly remembered that when I was about five, she'd tried to do this same thing for me, in Mama's bedroom, except that since she really didn't have a clue, I ended up looking like a circus clown.

I saw myself in that mirror, my blouse looking like I'd just come from a shift at the meat-packing plant, my hair all messed up from tussling with Lou, and there's Nikki, my creation, looking prettier than I'd even imagined she could. Turning, she brought her face right up against mine and kissed me. At first, I was scared — I thought about those gangster movies where you get kissed and then you get killed, and a part of me tensed and waited for the knife to come plunging in. I closed my eyes.

She kissed like a boy, though not like Lou, who'd made it feel like some kind of athletic event, or even like Troy Gray, who was much more romantic, but always seemed to be putting on an act. It was Troy's brother, Graham, I thought of, that gentle urgency, as if somewhere deep inside a door had been thrown open behind which there was more heat and light than you'd ever imagined. About a million thoughts ran around in my head, voices shouting how this was weird, unnatural, dangerous. I wondered if it was even happening at all, because with my eyes closed, it could have been anybody, really, and maybe I wasn't here and this wasn't Nikki I was with. Her hard, strong body was pressed up against mine, her mouth tasting vaguely of mint and toast, and she was kissing me, and I was kissing back. Somewhere in the distance, a train whistle blew.

After a while we stopped and just held each other. She ran the back of her hand up and along the side of my neck. I found the scar on her shoulder from the operation, ran my fingers along its contour and almost cried.

"Are you mad at me?" I asked.

"Hell," she said. "I'm not mad." She gave my neck one final kiss, then went to the refrigerator and got a beer. "I'm just trying to figure out what happens next."

"What do you mean? Next is our psych test. And you've got chem next week, don't forget." I sat down at the kitchen table, suddenly aware that I was sweating.

"I don't think so, Kare. I'm going to travel, I guess. I've got my loan money, and there's still time to get a partial tuition rebate — I checked. I hate to let you down like this, but I'm just not nursing material. I mean, imagine me in one of those white uniforms. 'Excuse me, sir, but it's time for your medication.' Hell, I'd be awful." She shook her head and smiled. "You go on without me."

"But what *will* you do?"

"I'll be fine. Don't worry."

I cleaned up and got ready for bed. I knew she was probably right, the nursing college wasn't looking at much less than a 3.0 for admission anyway, and Nikki's chances of getting that were slim. Even so, I felt pretty bad. Yowzer was prowling the counter, taking an occasional lick at the empty milk saucer, so I gave him some more, then went to my room and lay down. I could hear Nikki doing things out there, the television on softly to one of those program-length commercials.

It was as if my emotions were this big tangled ball of yarn, and while I could follow a thread for a few inches, I then lost it entirely. I wondered what she'd hoped would happen this evening. Thinking about her outfit and makeup just made me feel sadder. I thought about the coach at St. Mary's and wondered if what I'd done to her was just as bad.

After a while, the door to my room clicked softly open.

"Hey, Karina?" she said. In the light from the living room that silhouetted her in my doorway, I could see she'd changed back into jeans and a T-shirt. "You want to go for a ride?"

———

It was October, and the air had a crisp chill to it, but not so much that it didn't feel good against your face, and it smelled like autumn. I held on tight around her waist, the heat from the engine warming the inside of my ankles, watching the boxy houses zip past us in a long ribbon. I leaned into turns when she shouted for me to, but other than that we didn't talk, we just rode. We went out past a trailer park, then turned onto a road that had a lot less houses on it, where she cranked the engine and popped us up into another gear. It almost felt as if we were flying.

Soon we were out near the reservoir, and I thought maybe we'd stop there, but she kept on. About a mile further, she turned up a driveway, and at the end of it killed the engine. I heard an owl whoop in the distance, as if announcing our arrival. The stars were bright and clear against the sky, and you could see the Milky Way, too, woven like pipe smoke among them.

We were in front of a house, or rather, a house-in-progress. It had been framed out, and there were floors, but that was about it. I followed Nikki up a plank that served in the place of stairs.

"I figure this is going to be the kitchen," she said. "Stove over here, fridge there." She ducked through what was going to be a wall and into a larger area and held her arms out, demonstrating. "Living room. One hell of a view, too."

Looking down through the trees, I realized that we were only about twenty yards away from the lake, which lay out in the moonlight like an enormous, flat, black stone.

"Here you've got your master bedroom," she said, moving on to another area, "also with a view. Over here I figure is a guest room, or maybe a study. What do you think?"

"Study," I said. I found it hard to believe that she could look at these empty spaces and see anything at all.

"Me too. Over here's the master bathroom. There's another over there, but that'll just be a powder room, I guess. It's not big enough for a tub, or even a shower."

"Do you come out here often?" I asked.

"I don't know. A couple times a week. I like to see what kind of progress they're making. It's going to be a really nice house."

"It is. It's going to be a great house."

"I don't suppose I'll ever live anyplace like this."

She said it matter-of-factly, exactly the way, a few years earlier, when she'd discovered that at five-foot-five she'd stopped growing, she'd said to me, "I don't suppose I'll ever be any taller than this."

"Yes you will, Nikki," I said, now. "If you want to."

"Look," she said, "over here. This is going to be sliding glass doors, leading out onto a deck."

We sat there on the deck for a while and drank a couple of beers that Nikki had brought along, staring silently out at the lake, listening to the owl and the cicadas and the occasional liquid sound of a fish coming to the surface. I wanted to give her that house. But of course, a year from now, someone else would be sitting here. I wondered who they would be, whether they'd appreciate it even half as much as my sister, who knew every rib and bone, who'd watched it and lived in it before it was even there.

The wind shook the trees overhead, dropping a few acorns noisily onto the floor of the deck. Nikki picked one up and tossed it out into the water, where it fell with a tiny splash, and I remembered how I used to watch her in her blue-and-white softball uniform, rocketing the ball to third base after tagging some girl out at first, the power in her arm, the intensity in her eyes, the way the whole world seemed to revolve around her. I saw myself in that memory, too, sitting alone in the bleachers, a quiet girl with small eyes and a thin mouth, staring out into the sun and the dust, full of love and envy.

# THE HANDSTAND MAN

J imi-John Houser, bare chested and ripped jeaned, one sneaker laceless, toted sand up the steps to his fifth-floor walk-up. He was on his third sack, and the sweat formed rivers down his back, pooled in the band of his underwear. He'd stolen the sacks from a construction site three blocks away, and every minute of the agonizing journey back over sun-baked sidewalks, he had expected a hand on his shoulder, a shout, a police officer. But he would get away with this, it seemed.

Inside, he fell to his knees and shoved the sack next to the other two, then crawled over to the tiny refrigerator Jenny had rented for him last month when she'd arrived. He sucked gratefully from a two-liter, ninety-nine cent bottle of orange soda, until the fizz caught in his nose and he sputtered, choking on the sweet liquid.

His door creaked open and the little girl from downstairs came in, carrying a water balloon. She was six, with dark eyes and olive-colored skin. On her feet she wore pink basketball sneakers, the laces undone.

"Don't even think about it, Celeste," said Jimi-John. "I'm too busy to play games."

She sat down cross-legged on the floor, the balloon in her lap. "What are you doing?" she asked.

"Redecorating," he said. "Hey, your shoelace is untied."

"Where's all your stuff?"

He went over to her and picked her up under the arms, at which she began to giggle. "Out," he said. "Come back some other time to visit, señorita." Taking her into the hall, he placed her gently, still giggling, on her feet, and shut his door.

With his pocketknife, he cut open the first sack and dumped its contents onto the floor. It wasn't exactly what he'd hoped for—beach sand, smooth, blonde crystals baked dry by the sun. This was a coarser variety, browner in color, a little damp to the touch. But it made a nice pile, and after spreading it around a bit with his foot, Jimi-John decided that it would dry out satisfactorily by this evening.

———

The previous summer, just out of a job packing boxes for a toy manufacturer, he had taken his harmonicas, a change of clothes and a New York Mets baseball cap, emptied his savings account of nine-hundred and eighty-three dollars, and bought a round-trip ticket to Paris, France. From there he'd hitchhiked south, down through the wine country, eventually stopping in Perpignan at a hostel, where he fell in with an Australian who was traveling by motorcycle, also alone. They drank quantities of cheap wine daily, starting at noon. The Australian said that Jimi-John, with his new beard and skinny, six-foot frame, looked like a Byzantine Jesus. Together they had listened to the ocean slap at the coastline, lived entirely on fresh-baked bread and tins of pâté, and composed hit songs they could remember none of when they were sober. After a week they left for Barcelona, camping in fields at night, drinking heavily all the while. But when they got there the Australian announced he wanted to visit a mate of his in London. In front of a shop displaying colorful baskets of fake brand-name toothpaste and soap with labels that read "Gleam," and "Ivorey," they shook hands and said good-bye.

Immediately, Jimi-John felt lonely, even nostalgic for the good old days by the beach. Barcelona was too dirty, too loud. On the street below the window of his hotel room, vendors sold caged birds and monkeys that screamed. He took a train south along the coast, and got off in Sitges, choosing the resort town mostly because it was not too far away, and therefore an inexpensive ticket.

On the train he met three American girls, all of them nineteen, and at the station they banded together in search of housing. A bald-headed man named Pepé convinced them to come look at his cabaña, and they followed him through the sunlit streets, past white stucco houses, uphill to a quiet residence with three separate bedrooms and an inner courtyard. The girls' names were Jenny, Karen, and Chris. They wanted to make spaghetti for dinner, but found that only salt water came out of the taps, so instead they ate bread and cheese and drank wine, and afterward, Jimi-John passed out harmonicas, and they all played at once, in different keys.

Jenny was the one he liked, and she seemed to like him. They took walks together through the town, and she told him she was from Michigan, and considering going into theater. She said this as if somewhere out there, contracts existed that merely awaited her signature. She had marble-blue eyes, brown hair that seemed constantly to be in motion around her shoulders, and a small star of David, a gift from an old boyfriend, which she wore in one ear. Her voice was low and serious, and she seemed to Jimi-John years older even than he was. Jimi-John told her why he was called that — to distinguish him from his older brother James Roy, who was dead now anyway, a victim of the war. She'd been born the same year he died. On the beach in front of a boarded-up hotel, she calmly pulled her T-shirt over her head, revealing to him her small, pale breasts, and he felt honored. As she stretched out a few feet away from him, basking in the Spanish sun, Jimi-John was sure he'd never been happier.

———

He sliced open the next bag, took it by the corners and dumped out its contents. Now there were two big piles of sand on the floor. It was not a large apartment, just the one room. His window looked out on another building, a mirror image of this one, except that it was abandoned — a burnt-out shell. Jimi-John could look right into what used to be the apartment across from his. There seemed to be plants growing inside. Jungle over there, he thought, beach in here. Theme living.

He cut open the third and final bag. All the sand together covered the floor fairly well, but it wasn't very deep. Still, it would have to do. He didn't have the energy to steal more.

———

After Sitges, Jenny split off from her two friends, and she and Jimi-John traveled together, spending long, romantic evenings in tiny pensione bedrooms. They headed north toward Switzerland because she wanted to see the Alps. She'd been there once before, when she was little, on vacation with her parents. In Lucerne, low on funds and struck by an idea, he fashioned a harmonica holder out of two wire clothes hangers, then went down by the lake where the tourists congregated, stood on his hands and wheezed out a tune. While he drew their attention, Jenny passed through the crowd collecting francs in Jimi-John's baseball cap, filling it nearly to overflowing with gleaming silver.

They repeated this over the next few days, always to good crowds. In between they spent a lot of time just walking around. Jenny took photographs of Pilatus, trying to capture the way the light clung to the mountain at the end of the day, gold and then red and then almost blue. At the bank, their coins were dumped into a counting machine that digested them noisily, spitting out the occasional lire or deutschemark. An expressionless teller would pass them a handful of notes.

In Zurich, Jenny bought a couple of small cymbals for him to tie to his shoes, so that he could smash his feet together every now and then for added effect. She collected even more money, exercising a subtle charm as she moved unnoticed among the crowds that gathered to watch the upside-down harmonica player. Everyone gave her at least something. Inverted, Jimi-John watched with growing admiration. He became convinced that of the two of them, she was the one with the real talent. His arms grew stronger; at first he'd only been able to play one song before righting himself and resting. Now he could do three or four.

"Bonnie and Clyde," said Jenny, making a gun with her fingers and poking him in the ribs. "You distract them, I stick them up."

Together they learned the fine points of busking, how to move quickly into the midst of a crowded restaurant or outdoor café, play a song while collecting money at the same time, then leave before the management kicked them out. Jimi-John was a reasonably good harmonica player. He stuck to recognizable melodies — "Oh, Susanna," Beethoven's "Ode to Joy," some basic blues patterns, and a version of "Amazing Grace" people seemed to enjoy. What he lacked in ability, he made up for in sheer exuberance. Sometimes he wore the cymbals on his ankles even when he wasn't doing his act, just because it made people look.

"You've got them in the palm of your hand," Jenny told him. "They think you're crazy. They want to see what you'll do next."

"Either that, or they're waiting for me to tip over," he said.

They traveled more. In Salzburg, Jimi-John walked back and forth on his hands in front of Mozart's birthplace, playing "I'm an Old Cowhand."

"Come live with me," he said later as they counted their schillings at an outdoor café, taking turns tossing the worthless groschen out into the street.

"In New York?"

"In my apartment." He pictured the two of them tucked into a big double bed, reading books, sipping coffee. The apartment he pictured wasn't his own.

"Maybe in the spring," she said, flicking away one of the small coins.

"Really?" He wondered if this were actually happening, or if he would wake up in the morning and still be where he was two months ago, lying on his bed, timing the intervals between the trains that shuddered distantly underneath his apartment. He examined the red-and-white checked tablecloth for clues that it was not real. A gust of wind blew a piece of paper up against his leg and he shook it loose.

"We ought to think about going back soon," said Jenny. "It's starting to get cold."

"Back to the pensione?" he asked.

She put a hand on his and squeezed. "Back to the States."

———

All during the freezing winter, he'd nursed his love for Jenny. She sent him a picture or herself riding a horse, and although his favorite thing about her, her hair, was covered up by a riding cap, he taped it to the door of his broken refrigerator. He and his landlord were at a deadlock — the landlord didn't fix the appliances or provide enough heat, so Jimi-John didn't pay his rent, which of course meant that the landlord didn't fix the heat, etcetera. He did have hot water, though, and what food he needed to keep cold he placed on the window ledge, which was just about the right temperature, although milk tended to ice up. The refrigerator he filled with the paperbacks he read, mysteries mostly. Jimi-John wrapped himself in blankets and fed himself on memories of Sitges, Lucerne, Salzburg. It didn't seem possible he had lived such a life, only to return to this cave.

For money, he found a job in a record store that paid four dollars an hour, off the books. Everyone he worked with claimed to be a struggling musician. They complained constantly about "the Business," as if the only reason they weren't already famous and successful was that a huge conspiracy existed to keep art from the people. They weren't interested in hearing Jimi-John's stories of how he had actually been, for a short while, a self-supporting musician, performing in all the great cities of Europe. Instead, they ignored him. In their trendy clothes, they shook their heads as they discussed producers and labels and new artists, dropping the names to each other so indifferently they might have seen these people just the other night for drinks.

Jenny came at the beginning of June, a lavender suitcase in one hand, a dress bag over her other shoulder. Jimi-John met her at the airport, wearing a limo-driver's outfit he'd bought at Goodwill, carrying a sign with her name on it. He thought it would be a good joke, but wasn't prepared for what happened, which was that she walked right past him. He had to actually go over and touch her on the shoulder before she realized.

"Oh, I get it," she said. "A disguise."

At his apartment they hugged and made love, but he could tell right off that something wasn't right. Where in Europe she'd clung to him, digging her fingers into his back as if holding on for dear life, now she seemed distracted. She'd cut her hair too, and he had to get used to looking at her all over again. They talked about old times, and Jenny showed him her slides, which they had to hold up in front of a light bulb to view. Many of the pictures were of him, bearded and frazzled-looking, but still glowing with good health. He barely recognized himself. They talked about maybe writing a book together. Standing naked in front of the mirror, they examined their bodies—Jenny had lost her tan; Jimi-John had lost a lot of weight.

While he worked at the record store, she set about fixing up his place. She rented a small refrigerator, cleaned up the stove, put flowers in his drinking glasses, hung bamboo shades over the windows, where before he'd had only dirty blinds. It was a transformation, if a small one.

She enrolled in an acting school in the theater district and walked around evenings with a cork between her teeth saying things like "riding, on a bicycle," to practice her elocution. When her mother called on Sunday mornings, he had to be very quiet, since the story was that she had her own place. One night he got out a harp and blew a few bars of blues for her, but all she did was smile at him in a sort of forced way, which he found annoying.

Finally, after less than a month, she announced that she was bored.

"It isn't what I expected," she said.

Jimi-John was defensive. He'd just returned home, bringing

with him Chinese takeout for the third time that week. It was expensive, but it was her favorite.

"Give it some time," he said.

"I don't know," she said, bending down to touch her toes. "I've never lived with anyone before. I'm not sure I like it."

"We were together twenty-four hours a day for two months," he pointed out.

"But not this way. This place is a box. Everywhere I move, I bump into you. I don't want to live in a cage. Before, we were always moving from place to place. We had to figure out where to stay, what to eat." She unbent and faced him. "It was an adventure."

"This is an adventure too," said Jimi-John. "All you have to do is look at it that way." He pulled open the refrigerator. "Look, books in the Frigidaire."

Moving to the table, she sat down, pushed a couple newspapers out of the way and opened one of the cartons. A pungent Chinese food smell bloomed in the small room. She dumped Szechuan beef out onto a plate, then added a clod of rice. With a fork she stirred the food in slow, careful circles.

―――

Taking off his shoes, Jimi-John walked barefoot through the sand over to the closet, inside of which he had stored the inspiration for the whole production. A six-foot palm tree, left standing at the curb by some people who had moved. He'd come across it last week and known immediately what he would do.

Inside the closet also was a can of sky blue paint he'd had mixed specially and a roller and pan. He took them out, spread some newspaper, pried the top off the paint and stirred it. Then he went to work on the walls.

As he painted, he did his best to conjure up the memory of the beach at Sitges, the warm sun, the light breezes, the incredible blueness of a sky that seemed like a silk canopy high over their heads. The dingy, off-white of the walls slowly disappeared under his roller, though the new color was not all that he'd hoped for. A little too aquarium, he thought. A few drops fell at his feet, flecking the sand with tiny pearls that, were it not for their blueness, would have looked a lot like blood.

———

When Jenny moved out, she left him an explanatory list, printed neatly in pencil. Number one was age. His being ten years older, she felt he was looking for a commitment that she was not yet ready to make. Number two was lack of direction, something she'd never had before, but felt she was picking up from him. Number three had to do with the way he left the towels in the bathroom, and messiness in general. Number four was the neighborhood, which on top of being dangerous, she found downright depressing. Number five was her options, which she wanted to keep open. "I don't feel great about this," she wrote, "but it seems like better now than in six months." She was going to move in with a friend from her acting class who had a place in Astoria.

He called the phone number she left, and a man answered. "Oh," Jimi-John said, as if he'd just pushed open the wrong bathroom door. He hung up and stared at the number, then tried again. The same person answered. He put the receiver down and stared again at the list.

For two days he did not go to work, and when on the third, he did manage to get himself onto the subway and across town, he found that he'd been fired. He wasn't particularly surprised — it came as a kind of relief. Standing in the middle of the sidewalk, disrupting the steady flow of pedestrians like a rock in a streambed, he thought of his friend the Australian. He wished the two of them could get together again over a bottle of wine and a baguette, make up a few song lyrics, tell the rest of the world to bugger off.

When Shahim came by to drop off eviction papers, Jimi-John took it as a sign. "I'm not even going to fight," he told him.

"Not fight?" repeated the Turkish handyman, momentarily perplexed. Then he shrugged. "Stupid, anyway, to fight."

"The place is a dump," said Jimi-John. "It always will be."

"No," said Shahim. "Will be co-ops." He grinned, showing teeth stained yellow with tobacco.

Jimi-John took the papers and closed the door. It was finished now. A chapter coming to a close. What he needed was a fitting ending.

———

Jenny arrived at eight o'clock, wearing baggy shorts and an oversized T-shirt. He'd been waiting since seven, reading the first page of an old novel over and over, unable to make any real sense out of the words. "My God," she said when she saw the apartment.

The walls glistened with the still-wet paint. The palm tree stood in front of the window, framed by the vegetation in the abandoned apartment behind it. Jimi-John had read about this in an article somewhere, it was called borrowed landscape — stealing some distant view and making it your own. He'd spread the sand evenly across the floor, and in the middle he'd set out two towels.

"Piña colada?" he asked her. "I made a whole pitcher full. They're in the fridge."

"Which is in my name, incidentally," she said. "I've been meaning to remind you."

"It's a year since Pepé's," said Jimi-John. "Exactly a year this week."

"And you decided to destroy your apartment to celebrate?"

"Use your imagination. Pretend it's the beach."

They sat together on the towels and had drinks. Jenny told him about the play she was working on, not as an actress, but as a props person. "It's set in the punk period," she said. "I have to comb the secondhand stores looking for stuff. And we don't have a very big budget. I bought some barbed wire yesterday that was four dollars a foot."

"That's a lot," he said, nodding.

"You know, when you called me, I kind of thought you might be mad." She looked at him with an earnestness. "But you don't seem like you are."

"No." He lay back on his blanket and looked up at the ceiling, admiring the job he'd done. The color was even, the roller strokes all in the same direction. "I'm thinking about going back," he said. "Not immediately, I mean, I'll need to save a little while to get up the money. But in a month or two, you know?" He paused, unsure whether he wanted to meet her eyes.

•

She sipped her drink. "You really are crazy," she said. She scooped some sand up in her hand, let it drain slowly back down onto the floor. "I'm staying put, at least for a while."

He was surprised to find that this didn't really disappoint him. It was as if the place in him that had ached for her all this time had grown so large that, like an expanding star, it had given up all its energy. Instead, he felt only a quiet, spinning coolness.

They lay in silence on their blankets, listening to the sounds of traffic from the street below, savoring the light movement of air that came with the occasional breeze through the window. Nothing in particular happened. They were comfortable as long as they didn't talk.

"I should get going," she said. "I'm meeting someone in a half-hour."

"Whatever," said Jimi-John.

When they stood he tried a kiss, but she slipped her head to one side, presenting him only her cheek. Then she wrapped her arms around him and hugged him as she might have an older brother. She reached up and gave him a tug on the ear, and left.

Alone again, he wondered, just for a second, what had happened to him. The blueness of the walls seemed so obvious, so calculated. They were after all, still walls, not open air. The palm tree stood stupidly in the sand. It had seemed all along such a brilliant idea, but now, feeling as disconnected as the cord dangling from his toaster, it occurred to him that he had no place to go and no particular goals. When he was in Barcelona, he remembered, a monkey had escaped from one of the vendors' cages. It ran around in circles a few times screaming with glee, attempted to cross the road and almost got hit. With nowhere else to go, it scampered back onto the median with all the other caged monkeys, then clambered to the top of a tree where it stayed, occasionally hurling debris down at its owner. That's about the level I'm at, he thought. He tossed his empty piña colada glass out the window, waited to hear it smash.

His doorknob turned and he went to unlock it. It was Celeste. "Mira," she said. "A beach."

"Go on," he told her. "It's too late for you to be wandering around. Where's your mama?"

"Watching TV." She ran over to the tree and grabbed its thin trunk. "What's this?"

"It's a dum-dum tree," said Jimi-John.

"No it isn't."

"Yes it is. It's a very stupid plant. It only grows in warm climates, but you can fool it, as I have done here, by making it think it's at the beach."

"What did you do with all your stuff?" she demanded, wandering further around the apartment.

"All gone. I'm going to move away."

"How far?"

"I don't know yet."

She found his harmonica case in the corner with his shoes and clothes, and dumped them out in front of her. He went over and picked up two, giving one to her.

"Plants like music," he said. "But a dum-dum tree doesn't like just any kind of music. It has to be dumb music."

She raised one eyebrow skeptically at him. She seemed about ready to put the harmonica down. Positioning the instrument in his mouth, Jimi-John put his hands to the floor and flipped his legs up over his head. His first thought was that his arms had grown weak, because they trembled under his weight, but then he found a balance point and they held. His body was considerably thinner than it had been the last time he'd tried this, so it wasn't so hard. Blood rushed to his head.

Without his holder, he could do little more that blow in and out of the harp, but that was enough to amuse Celeste. She screamed with pleasure, put the other harmonica to her lips and began playing. Jimi-John hand-walked his way over to the palm, where his feet came just about even with the top of the tree. The sound of the two harmonicas was delicious and discordant, like a hilariously out-of-tune pipe organ. He lowered himself and rested on his back in the sand.

Celeste poked at him with her finger. "More," she said.

"I don't know, kid."

"More."

He cast his eyes around the room. "Look," he said. "You go downstairs now. If you do that, I'll make you a deal. You come back tomorrow morning and you can help me paint the sand blue."

"Blue!" she screamed.

"So the dum-dum tree thinks it's near water. OK?" He stuck out his hand and they shook on it. Then he hoisted her over his shoulders and hiked down to the second floor, where the sounds of a loud TV filtered out into the hallway. He deposited her in front of her door.

"Don't forget," he said. "Bright and early."

"I saw your girlfriend," she confided.

Standing alone in the dimness, surrounded by closed doors and the phantom hallway smells of cleaning solution, urine, other peoples' suppers, he wondered if he should just keep going. Tomorrow he would be rootless again anyway. He tried to imagine himself disappearing into the folds of the city, which had been all along his general plan, but right now seemed hugely inadequate. He considered taking a bus to the suburbs, hitching to the interstate and heading west, but this, too, depressed him — he had a good enough idea about California to know he didn't want to be there. For a moment he stood, leaning in both directions at once, unsure whether to go down the stairs or up, not exactly feeling sorry for himself, more confused.

Sitting down on one of the worn stone steps, he closed his eyes tight and thought about his brother, James Roy, lying boxed and still beneath the North Carolina earth. When the news came, he'd been at first stunned and sad — he was barely thirteen, had never known anyone who'd died. Just plucked out of life, silently, like they'd never really been there at all. Then, slowly, a kind of amazement had set in at the very fact of his own existence. The most ordinary things impressed him. The sun coming through his bedroom window, the way his heart continued to beat all by itself. Stop signs and trees and glasses of milk — for a few weeks they were all equally remarkable. The world had seemed lit from within by a fragile light.

Behind the door to Celeste's apartment, the television suddenly grew quiet. Someone was putting her to bed now, wondering, per-haps, just what it was the little girl was smiling about. Jimi-John stood and smacked his hands against his jeans to rid them of the dust. For tonight at least, he would sleep on his own private beach, wake up with sand in his shoes.

# BIG GREY

I t was Tony's idea to go after Big Grey. We hanging out back at the place, me reading some old comic books I got laying around and Tony practicing his guitar. It's an electric one, Tony's guitar, all black and silver. He got it from a junkie in Canarsie who carved the names of all the notes into the side of the neck. Looks like a bird walked along there. Probably took the dude hours, but he sold it anyway when things got tight and he found himself staring at that wall, which will happen. Tony play it through his box. He got this cord and he just plug it right in the back of the radio. His playing ain't much to talk about, not yet, but he be practicing and practicing, and you work at a thing that hard, something bound to come of it.

So Tony trying to play something, some tune off the radio, and I'm reading this old Spiderman I read about a million times before, and suddenly Tony puts down the guitar and stands up and says let's head on down to the park.

I says why. It's dark out already, and too damn cold to be drinking no beer out there. But Tony already up and moving all around the place, looking under chairs, behind the sofa, in all the closets. Finally he say "aha!" and come out with a big old softball bat, weighted aluminum. He raise it up, get the feel of it, then send an imaginary one over the center field wall.

"What you want that for?" I ask him.

"Big Grey," he say. "We going hunting."

It's funny, but sometime I have trouble telling when Tony messing around or telling the truth. But he grinning and his eyes looking all fired up and so I didn't ask no questions. I just said let's go, and we went.

Big Grey is this old dog we see almost all the time over in the park. It's a big old German shepherd with a hurt paw, meaner than hell. He run with a pack of strays that live over there, but most of them keeps their distance from Grey, because they scared of him. He got this old scroungy bitch that stay right by his side, a shepherd like him, and she mean, too, though I think it's mostly just fear. She'll growl and bark at you, then jump back a few feet where you can't get her and bark and growl some more. I thrown a stick at her one time and she run. But Grey be another thing — that boy come at you like he mean business.

It's cold out and the park is dead empty. The moon is shining though, and it feels good to be outside. We finds some ducks wandering around and chases them back into the water. Tony keeps the softball bat resting on his shoulder, every now and then swinging it like a cop spinning his nightstick. I picks up a part of a branch off the ground and break the twigs off it until it's a club. Just holding it I feel like king of the world. Sticks is funny like that — it feels good to carry one.

So we head on up to the graveyard, back in the woods. It's up on a hill and fenced off from the rest of the park, and the strays like to hang back there. That's where you usually see them — if you cutting through the park sometimes they come running at you all barking and going crazy. I hold my stick tighter and follow Tony. He's not talking and I'm beginning to wonder if he's on something. But I don't say nothing. He got his moods just like everyone else, I guess.

Up by the graveyard Tony start poking around in the dead leaves, looking for something. He muttering to himself and pushing around with the end of the softball bat, and suddenly he bend down and bring up about a half a bottle of wine.

"See, I was up here this afternoon," he say.

"By yourself?" I say.

"And that crazy dog chase me all the way down to the baseball fields."

It makes me laugh picturing Tony dropping his wine and shooting down the hill chased by a big hungry dog. But Tony don't laugh.

"Got to get even," he say.

I try to laugh like it's a joke, but Tony got this real serious look on his face, so I stops quick. We drink some of the wine, not saying much, keeping our eyes out for Big Grey. But no sign of him, and after a while drinking Tony start to loosen up. When the wine just about gone, he start faking like he playing the guitar, doing that song I heard him practicing, throwing in a few moves. So I start to get into it, playing drums in the air and making the noises with my mouth. We got a pretty nice jam going right there underneath the trees. Then all of a sudden, Tony stop moving and point.

At first I don't see nothing, then I do. He just standing there watching us, maybe ten yards off. It's so dark you can't hardly see him, just mostly his eyes, yellow and mean, almost looking like they floating by themselves in the air. I can hear him growling, soft and low.

Tony whisper to me that we going to surround him. I about to ask how we going to do that with only two of us, but he already gone, slipping from tree to tree, sneaking off to the side so he can come up behind Big Grey. Tony can be real quiet when he want to. Sometime, back at our place, he can come in so quiet you don't even know he there, until you look up and he in a chair opening up some beer. He's nearly given me a couple of heart attacks. Me, I can't take a piss without the whole world hearing me flush.

Well, I'm holding my stick so tight my hands are beginning to hurt, and I see that dog start moving on me, real slow with a little limp from his busted paw, and the next thing I know, I'm running on down the hill. At the bottom I turns around and see that he stopped about halfway down, looking at me and barking, showing those yellow teeth and pacing back and forth like he marking out his turf. Then I hear a yell, and there's Tony with the baseball bat over his head running down on the dog and shouting like a crazy man. I think the dog more surprised than me, because he spin around full circle and practically fall over, then hop on down the hill toward me.

Now we both running, me and Big Grey. They got baseball fields in the park, with big fences around them to keep foul balls in, and being a little drunk and a lot scared, I run smack into one. I bounce right off it and land in the dirt. I don't bother to get up, just cover my head with my hands and close my eyes tight. The way I see it, I'm dog food.

But after a few seconds when I still don't feel no teeth on my neck I get up and look. Tony and Big Grey faced off just a few feet away, and the dog got his back to me. I picks up my stick. Tony stepping toward Big Grey, and Grey growling. I don't know why, but right then I throws my stick at the dog. I guess I just don't want to see him get Tony. I don't really think about it, I just throws it.

Well, I miss, but I make him jump and turn to see what it is, and Tony take two steps forward and swing. The bat make a soft noise, like a thump, and catch Big Grey right under the ear. He start walking around in circles, just going around and around in the same spot, maybe like ten or fifteen times. Finally he lie down.

"You shouldn't have done that," Tony say.

"Done what?" I still got my eyes on Big Grey. Any second now I expect him to jump up and attack. But he lay still.

"Distract him. It wasn't fair."

"Don't blame me," I says. "You the one that hit him."

But Tony down on one knee now, inspecting the dog. I come over to him, pick up my stick and give him little poke, but he don't move. I tell Tony I think he dead.

"He ain't. He's breathing."

Well, he breathing all right, but after the way Tony busted on him, I know it won't be for long. But I don't say nothing, I just nod.

I'm about ready to say let's head down to the social center for some pinball, because this ain't turning out to be so much fun. Then I see Tony picking up Big Grey in his arms.

"You crazy?" I says. "What you want to do with him?"

"C'mon," Tony say. "There's a vet up on Sixth Street."

Believe it or not, we does it between the two of us, but it's killin' work. Big Grey must weigh about eighty or ninety pounds, and he don't smell none too good. But we get him up the path and out the parkside. We find the vet.

This a pretty fancy vet, and when we walks in with a big ugly dog that look like he dead, and us definitely not looking like we from the neighborhood, we turns a few heads. It's mostly cats in the waiting room, two in carry cases and one in this dude's lap. And then there's this skinny, rich-looking lady with a little white dog that's got a bright, pink bow on. She's eyeballing us pretty good and probably dialing 911 in her head. I give her a big smile and go up to the desk.

It's an emergency see, I tell the lady, our dog got hit by a car. I'm not about to tell them the truth because they might call the ASPCA or something. Lady give me a look like she wishing she never come in this evening, then say, OK, take him into this room that's just off the waiting room. So I call Tony and we move old Grey into this tiny room and lay him down on the floor.

They keeps us waiting quite a while. Tony being real quiet, just sort of staring down at his sneakers. Big Grey laying on his side, but his eyes open and he watching us. The room got a strong hospital smell that make it hard to breathe. Seem like I'm the only one nervous at all, and I'm not even sure why I should be, but I keep on getting up and sticking my head out the door to see if the doctor coming or what. Finally they send some Jamaican dude in to take a look. He wearing a white coat, but I can see he ain't no doctor. He probably just some kind of assistant. There ain't no Jamaican doctors, not in this part of town.

Well, he get down on one knee and start poking around on Big

Grey. He look in his eyes and feel for his heartbeat. When he reach for his mouth and lift up his lips, I expect to see his hand get bit right off, but that dog just laying there without no fight in him at all. Only thing moving on him is his eyes, and they following the guy, every now and then looking over at us. Finally the dude say this dog got a serious problem.

I say we know that, why do he think we here? But he just shake his head. Say the best thing for everyone involved probably just be put him to sleep. That cost thirty-five dollars, fifty if we want to leave him there.

Then Tony on his feet. "What about an operation?" he say.

Operation very expensive, the man say. He doubt we have that kind of money. Besides, the dog looking like he too far gone for an operation anyway. Best thing be give him the injection. Get a new dog. Also he say Big Grey got a mess of other problems too, like mange, fleas, probably worms, and a couple of other things I don't quite catch. His paw busted too. Didn't we never take him to no vet before?

So I says excuse us, but we'd like to discuss this by ourselves for a minute. Then I tell Tony now we done it. It going to cost thirty-five dollars just to kill him off. I vote for taking him back to the park. If it got to be done, there's cheaper ways. The pond for instance.

Then the dude come back in and ask if we got any money for the injection. I tells him the truth, which is of course no. He shake his head and say I'm sorry, but we ain't running no welfare clinic, but maybe if we want to take him into the city they got an ASPCA clinic there that's free.

Tony say forget it, we going to take him back home and he lifting Big Grey back up in his arms again. He do it real gently, and he don't even seem to mind the stink. Jamaican dude shaking his head at us as we go out, like he thinking we shouldn't be allowed to own no dog anyway.

We swipes one of those shopping carts from out back of the Key Food so we won't have to carry him all the way back to our crib. Tony drop him in like a sack of onions and push him along, me helping when we come to curbs. We stop and pick up some beer too.

Finally we gets back and carry him up the stairs. Our place on the fourth floor and it never seem like as much steps as this time. We got a small place, but nice. Actually, it's Carla's brother's place, but he in jail right at this time and don't expect to be using it too soon. Carla is Tony's lady. She still live with her parents, but she over our place a lot too. Always some kind of party over our place, seems like.

Tony take a couple of towels and make a little bed for Grey in the middle of the floor and we arrange him on them so he looking comfortable. Dog seem just like he dead, except his eyes is wide open and he staring at us, watching what we up to.

"Try giving him some water," I says. "Maybe he's thirsty."

So Tony tries to give him some, but he ain't interested. We practically sticks his nose in it but he don't drink. Finally we gives up and Tony picks up his guitar and gets a beer. I get one too and try to get back into my comic book. But I have a hard time concentrating because I keep looking down and seeing that dog, and every time it seem to me like he looking right back, saying, "you responsible." Meanwhile Tony just doodling on the guitar, not playing nothing in particular, staring at the wall and just about driving me crazy with not talking.

About ten-thirty Carla come by with her friend Candy who works over at the Key Food. They bring by some more beer and smokes and a huge bag of Doritos. Both of them screams when they walks in the door. I start to laugh. Seem at least a little fun going to come out of this evening. Big Grey just blink his eyes.

It takes a couple of minutes, but we manages to calm the girls down, and I'm happy to see Tony seem to be coming out of it. He making jokes and drinking beer and nibbling around on the back of Carla's neck, and just generally starting to act like his old self. He say we throwing a special testimonial, with Big Grey the honored guest. Let's all drink his health.

We drink one to Big Grey. Then we drink another, and then another, and pretty soon we got us a party going. Tony unplug his guitar and put on some tunes. Couple other folks drops by around eleven, dudes from downstairs, and everyone want to dance with Candy, who looking particularly fine. All this while Big Grey just laying in the middle of the floor, but everybody just about forgets about him. Then one of the dudes from downstairs goes over and turns down the music. Without it on I can suddenly hear a noise out in the street. Some dog going crazy down there, howling like a wild animal.

The dude, whose name is Junior, says to Tony, "Man, you ought to take this thing out of here." He nudge Grey with his foot. "This dog is dead."

"Ain't dead," says Tony. "Just resting."

Junior say he don't know about that, the dog looking like he dead and he sure smelling like it too.

Tony say if Junior so uncomfortable with Big Grey around, maybe he ought to leave.

"Come on, Tony," Carla say, "A joke is a joke. Take him on out to the dumpster or something." She laugh like she made a joke. Outside, that dog still howling its head off.

Then Tony start to go crazy. Just crazy, like a wild man. He pick up his guitar and smash it against the wall, then spin around and hold it out in front of him and say everybody got to leave right now. Then he smack it down on the floor and say, go on, move.

Tony never love anything as much as that guitar, and now he busting it all to hell, which make me think no question but he serious. Everybody start to leave, but I hang around because me and Tony best friends, and besides I got no place to go anyway. Carla go up to him and try to put her arms around his waist, but he push her away and smack the guitar against the coffee table, knocking over three or four cans of beer which hit the floor gushing liquid like wounded men. Carla shaking her head and calling Tony crazy man and some other things, but finally she leave too, slamming the door behind her, and now we alone, me, Tony, and Big Grey.

Tony toss the guitar across the room and sit down. I don't know what to say, so I don't say nothing. We just sit there, quiet. Tony open up the last of the beers and take a swallow, then offer it to me. I drink some and put it down. Big Grey breathing a little different it seem to me, more difficult. He still laying in the same position as we put him in, on the towels on his side. Outside that dog still howling. It sound like someone beating it.

Then Tony ask me did I ever see this movie, *The Good the Bad and the Ugly*. I say yeah, I think so. But do I remember the part at the end where they all facing each other with guns drawn, and nobody want to shoot because no way he can win? I say I remember that part.

"It ain't never fair," says Tony.

"What?" I asks.

Then Tony tell me he think life a lot like that movie. Whatever you gonna do, someone else always got the drop on you. Somebody always got the advantage. It ain't good, or bad, just ugly.

I nod like I know what he talking about, then I look over at Big Grey. He starting to shake and breathe real heavy. Both of us watch him. It takes about thirty seconds, then it's over and he laying still. Now his eyes finally closed.

"Don't take it too hard," I say. "It ain't your fault."

But Tony not even listening to me, he just staring down at the dog, and I know he thinking it is. Seems to me now like maybe he ought to be alone, so I says I think I'll go out. Tony don't say nothing. Then I offer to help him take Big Grey out, maybe back to the park or something, but he still don't seem to notice I'm talking to him at all.

So I slips out the door and down the stairs. I'm feeling bad, real low. Tony acting so strange, it seem like he maybe never going to come out of it. I can see him in some kind of institution or something, not talking, getting meals fed to him, maybe just sitting around all day staring at the TV. I start to think maybe I'll try to hunt up Carla and together we'll go back in an hour or so and try to snap him out of it.

I open the door and steps out. It's cold, dark, and empty in the street, and the only sound is a humming from the streetlight over my head. Then I hear this whimpering.

I jump because I'm surprised, then I back away slow. It's Big Grey's bitch, almost as big as him, but skinny. You can count her ribs. She must have somehow followed us all the way home. I ain't never seen her anywhere outside of the park, and I wonder what she going to do now. Moving slow and easy, I cross the street, then when I got a safe distance between us I turn and watch her. She howling and pawing at the door. Somehow, from the smell I guess, she know Big Grey inside. She keep howling and pawing, and I figure pretty soon someone gonna call the cops and that be the end of her. Then, so quiet it might have been a ghost doing it, the door opens up. I stopped worrying so much about Tony after I seen him let that old bitch into the house.

# MAGISTER LUDI

D uney is on the phone with her best friend, Beth Ann, running down a list of all the boys in their senior class at Dover High, deciding which ones are or are not virgins. She sits at her kitchen table, wrapping the phone's long white cord around and around her arm as she talks. Her parents, who are away in the city for the rest of the afternoon, until late tonight, have left Duney, who is seventeen, in charge, and she has taken the opportunity to mix herself a tall drink and enjoy the luxury of a good long phone call.

It is muggy for early June, and her glass sweats long beads of water which she traces slowly with her index finger. Summer has come early this year, and she thinks it would be nice to climb right in there with the ice cubes. The girls have been talking over an hour, and her ear is getting a little strained, as is her enthusiasm for the topic. It is a kind of game with them; Duney will name someone, and Beth Ann gives her opinion. Then Beth Ann names someone else, and so on. They have played this a lot, to the point where sometimes, in the hallways at school for instance, when a boy passes by, all one of them has to do is say "yes," nod her head, and the other knows exactly what she means. Duney and Beth Ann are both virgins themselves, but they don't feel this makes them any less qualified as judges.

From the basement come loud, fragmented noises—the honk of a saxophone, a distorted, tortured note from an electric guitar. Duney's brother, Rick, is having band practice at their house this afternoon. Every now and then the screen door bangs open and another flush-faced kid enters carrying a piece of musical equipment. Rick is two years younger than Duney, and she has only a limited tolerance for him when he's with his friends.

"It's a macho thing," she tells Beth Ann, changing the subject, speaking loud enough to be overheard. "They wear tight pants and T-shirts and strut around like they're big shots. Music is the last thing on their minds." She sips at her drink and watches as a tall, acned blonde kid carrying a bass drum in front of him tries to maneuver his way through the door.

"Hey, hey, watch the walls," she shouts at him. "Jesus," she says into the phone, "you wouldn't believe what is going on over here."

When she hangs up, Rick is behind her waiting. "What are you drinking?" he asks.

"Rum and coke."

"Think I'll have one." Rick is cultivating a kind of sneering grin these days that Duney hates. It's all part of a new personality he's working on that she dates directly to his purchase of an electric guitar.

"Just keep your friends out of Dad's liquor cabinet. I noticed that bottle of B&B is almost empty."

"So what?" says Rick, pouring himself some rum into a glass. "He'll never notice. He hates the stuff. Have you ever tried it?" He makes a disgusted face and dumps Coca-Cola into his glass. It foams up over the edges, making a mess.

"Going to clean that up?"

"Yes, Boss!" He salutes then yanks about fifteen sheets of paper toweling off the roll and piles it all onto the spill. "Some friends are going to come over to check out the jam."

She shrugs. "So?"

"So nothing. I thought I'd let you know. What are you going to do?"

Duney knows he wishes she would leave, and it has in fact crossed her mind to do so. But she's not sure she wants to give him the pleasure of total freedom. With their parents gone, Duney is the last vestige of authority, and she worries about Rick.

"Somebody's got to stick around and make sure you don't burn the place down," she says.

"Right," says Rick.

Duney puts her feet up and pages through the local paper. The movies haven't changed since last week, and she's seen them both. The high school baseball team is on the verge of its worst season ever, having lost nine straight now. Beth Ann and she have taken an interest in the sport ever since they decided they like a guy on the team. His name is Roy, a tall, beanpole of a kid with red hair and incredibly sexy eyes. Duney and Beth Ann are both on the swim team, and sometimes after practice, they stop off to watch Roy. Eyes are Duney's thing—she's decided she can tell everything about people from their eyes, though she believes her own are inexpressive. Watching Roy is more of a joke with them than anything else. He's a junior, and realistically, Duney doesn't believe she could ever go out with someone younger than she is. She thinks of her brother's friends and shudders.

Downstairs, the music starts up at a volume so extreme it is as if a subway train is passing under the house. Duney gets up and walks into the living room, where the thick carpeting muffles the sound somewhat. Everything vibrates—the furniture, the walls—all pulse as if alive. She wishes Rick had taken up something more normal, like baseball, or devil worship. Heading for the liquor cabinet, she pours herself another drink, choosing bourbon this time, in an effort to make the levels in the bottles all decrease at a similar rate. A painting hangs crooked, possibly as a result of the music. She adjusts it and goes back into the kitchen where she pours Coca-Cola into her glass.

At the end of the summer Duney will be leaving for college, and this fact has recently begun to weigh upon her mind. She's found herself getting sentimental about the dumbest things: certain buildings in town that she's never been inside, an ancient bike rack that used to be as tall as she was, a particular section of cracked, heaved up sidewalk she's walked over a thousand times. Something inside her wants to hold on, to lock these things up forever where they'll be safe. She and Beth Ann have made a pact that whatever happens, no matter where they are, they will meet five years from now at the Jersey Shore where Beth Ann's parents have a cottage, and where they spent what they have both agreed was the best ten days of their lives last summer. But thinking back on it, Duney has trouble remembering what it was that made the trip so special. She remembers only a blur of hot sun, sandy towels, and endless, mindless conversations with boys. She wonders what it is they're hoping so much to preserve, and whether five years from now they'll be sorry they tried.

She opens the paper again and reads the police blotter. It is all petty stuff: tape decks stolen from cars, a window broken on campus in order to steal kegs of beer. Someone named Rufus Lemott from Trenton, arrested for possession of a firearm and a small amount of cocaine. She wishes something would really happen sometime. A bank robbery maybe, or a mob-style assassination. She imagines the headline — Organized Crime Figure Shot on Line at Burger King. That would shake things up a bit.

The screen door opens and two girls she recognizes as freshmen come in, bringing with them a powerful scent of strawberry perfume. They don't even look at Duney, but go straight for the basement door. Both wear halter tops and tight, tight jeans. Groupies, Duney thinks in amazement. My brother actually has groupies.

His band is called Magister Ludi, lifted from a Hesse novel Duney knows for a fact Rick has never read. He has taken a laundry marker and carefully inscribed the name on the back of his jeans jacket. He has also made a poster which adorns the door to his room, along with a sort of logo he's designed: three glass balls floating over a horizon. The poster isn't bad at all, but she wishes he'd ease up on the rock star act. His hair is almost down to his shoulders, and since he has no beard yet, only a bit of darkening fuzz over his lip, Duney thinks he looks like a girl. He marches around the house with his guitar around his neck at all times, beats out rhythms with his utensils on the dining table at meals, screams out lyrics in the shower. She tells him it is embarrassing. He accuses her of being just as bad as those conservative housewives who want to censor everything in sight, and though she denies it, she wonders. There seems no question that rock and roll is corrupting her brother.

She remembers Rick the way he used to be, always following her around, coming into her room to watch her do homework, sitting in silent admiration as she worked on math problems. They used to wrestle sometimes too — matches which she, being bigger, could have won, but would allow herself to lose at the last moment, just as Rick's frustration began to show in his reddened face, near tears. He had never been particularly bright, but he was a good kid, and she hates the way he is so obviously attempting to change his personality. He is acting tough, talking less, being surly and rude to their parents, and treating Duney almost as if she were younger than he. Sniffing the air, Duney detects a hint of marijuana drifting up from the basement. She shakes her head and goes back out to the living room. She hopes it's all just a phase.

A car pulls into their drive, and Duney looks out to see who it is. Most of Rick's friends are too young to drive, and she hopes this may be someone coming to visit her. But she has never seen the beat-up station wagon that parks outside, or the people who get out of it. There are four of them, big guys, all carrying beer, one with a guitar case. They enter the kitchen without knocking, just as Duney comes to the door.

"They're downstairs," she says, stating the obvious. These people are older — in their mid-twenties at least. They have long hair and smell strongly of beer. It is as if a motorcycle gang has stepped into her house.

One of them, in a torn T-shirt, with a mustache and a pock-marked face, grins at her. "Is that where they are?" he says.

"Are you friends of Rick's?" she asks. Maybe they have the wrong house.

He looks at the others. "Are we friends of Rick's?" The one carrying the guitar nods. Though he has said nothing, Duney gets the sense that he is in charge.

"That's right, we're friends of Rick's. Who are you friends of?"

"I *live* here." She does her best to seem unimpressed, turns and walks over to the table. "You can go downstairs." Picking up the newspaper, she pretends to read, but keeps one eye on them. When they open the basement door, it's almost like opening a blast furnace, the way the noise explodes into the kitchen.

She sits for a while, uncertain whether she has made a mistake allowing these people into her house, and a little angry that Rick didn't explain the people coming over weren't just kids. The music grinds to a halt, and a minute later Rick bursts up into the room. He starts rummaging in the cabinets.

"Who are those guys?"

"Friends," he says. "Didn't Mom buy any chips or peanuts, or anything?"

"Over there," she says, pointing. "Aren't they a little bit older than you?"

"I guess so. That one guy is Riggy. I might buy his guitar."

"Buy his guitar? You just bought yours."

"Well, trade maybe."

"What do you think Mom and Dad are going to say about that?"

"Lighten up, will you? I can do what I want. You're not them. Anyway, they mostly came to check out our band. They're professionals — they play all around. All the local bars."

This interests her. She knows the names of some of the local bands, mostly from Beth Ann, who keeps up with that kind of thing. "What are they called?" she asks.

"Jackal. Ever heard of them?"

She hasn't. She's been out to a few bars in town, but not ones where they have music. It's one of the things she imagines herself doing when she gets to college, going to bars and dancing all night. "I like the name," she says.

"It's all right." He discovers a bag of Cheetohs and seizes it. "I like our name better."

She feels like teasing him a little. "*Your* name is pretentious. Nobody is going to know what it means anyway. Jackal is much better. It's sleek, and a little angry sounding. A good rock-and-roll name."

He sticks a Cheetoh in his mouth and looks at her, obviously irritated. "What would you know about it anyway?" he says. "*You* like Elton John." Having dealt this blow, he retreats to the basement.

———

Duney walks around the house, feeling the vibrations under her feet, sipping at her drink. Though it's nearly supper time, she's not hungry at all, just very lightheaded. Going upstairs to her parents' bedroom, where she'll be able to hear better, she calls Beth Ann.

"It's me," she says. "What are you doing?"

"Setting the table," says Beth Ann. "You sound toasted."

"Maybe a little. I've had a few."

"Wish I could join you. How are things at Madison Square Garden? Any windows broken yet?"

"No, but listen. Some guys came over, older guys. They're in a group called Jackal. Ever hear of them?"

There is an audible gasp from the other end. "That's Riggy Banks's group. They're great! Well, I've never actually heard them, but they play around a lot. I think they even have a record. How come they're at your house?"

"Rick wants to trade guitars with him or something."

"I'd be careful if I were you. Those guys have a pretty wild reputation."

"Oh?" she says, running her hand along the surface of her parents' bed. It is made so neatly, there isn't the slightest wrinkle. "Do you think I ought to be worried?"

"Not worried, just careful. I don't know, if things get out of hand you could always ask them to leave. Or call the police."

"Beth Ann!"

"I'm just *kidding*. What are they doing?"

"Who knows? They're in the basement." Standing, she looks out her parents' window onto their driveway where the rusted station wagon sits, a misfit among the well-trimmed lawns, looking somehow ominous in the gathering shadows. "Why don't you come over?" she asks.

"I can't," says Beth Ann. "We're having dinner, and then I'm supposed to baby sit across the street. Listen, I've got to go. My Mom's shouting for me. I'll call you later from the Schanbergs'."

Duney goes into her own room and stands looking at it, biting at her thumbnail. She still has bunk beds. She has had them for so many years that she almost never thinks about them, but right now they look positively ridiculous to her. She wonders why she would have ever wanted them in the first place. For years she's been sleeping on the bottom bunk, ignoring the upper one entirely. But looking at it, she remembers vaguely that when she was younger she did sleep on top. It had felt like being an explorer to be so tiny and elevated to such a dizzying height. She remembers the sensations, but as if they belong to another person — a feeling of being high off the ground, able to reach out and almost touch the ceiling, of knowing what it was like to be in a place where no one, not even the grown-ups, ever went.

She decides to have a cigarette. She has a pack she keeps in her desk, and she takes one out and gives it a sniff. She knows cigarettes are supposed to get stale, which means that these, over a month old, are certainly candidates. But she smokes so rarely that she can't see it making a difference. How do people know their cigarettes are stale? It seems impossible to her that smoke should have such subtle qualities. If she smoked for years, she doesn't believe she'd be able to tell. Rummaging around, she finds she has no matches. She goes back downstairs. There are some in the kitchen, but first she pours a dollop of scotch into her glass. One of the kitchen drawers is full of matchbooks collected over the years from nearly every restaurant her parents have been to; since neither of them smoke, they are all untouched. Boring, she thinks, looking into the drawer, pushing the little boxes around with one finger. How incredibly boring. She closes it without taking out any matches, then, slipping the unlit cigarette between her lips, opens the basement door.

The downstairs has been transformed. Cigarette and reefer smoke mingle in a thick haze, and the air is ripe with the smell of perspiration, like a gym. The music has stopped for the time being, and people are hanging around everywhere. Duney had not realized what a crowd had come over — without counting, she guesses there are about fourteen bodies down here. Empty beer cans all over the place. Two of the guys from the station wagon are seated on the sofa, each with one of the halter-topped freshmen in his lap. The one with the pockmarked face leers at her, but she ignores him and goes over to where Rick is standing, looking, she thinks, very young in this company.

"How's it going?" she asks.

"Not bad," says Rick. "Do you need a light for that?"

She nods, feeling that for the moment some kind of gap has been bridged between them. Rick knows she could have lit the thing upstairs.

"Wait a minute." He goes over to the drum set, where the guy who had brought over the guitar is seated, spinning lazily back and forth on the drum stool, a guitar in his lap. Even before she hears Rick speak his name, she knows that this is Riggy. There is a kind of easy authority about him. She likes the way he smokes and plays at the same time, not even bothering to remove the cigarette from his mouth, just blowing smoke out one side. He stops playing and produces a lighter from his front pocket, which he hands to Rick, who brings it over to Duney and lights her cigarette for her.

"Thanks," she calls over to Riggy. He nods back. Duney decides he doesn't look dangerous at all. A little dirty maybe.

Rick pokes her arm. "How does it sound?"

"What?"

"The music, idiot. Do you think it sounds all right?"

Duney almost never says anything positive to Rick about his playing, for fear of encouraging him. But she is feeling magnanimous. "It sounded really good," she says. "I was amazed."

"Yeah?" For just a moment his mask drops and she thinks she

sees her real brother. But it is only for a second, and he quickly begins nodding his head to some inner beat, at the same time looking around the room in case anyone should notice him spending so much time with his sister.

"How come you stopped? Are you finished?"

"Just taking a break. We might all go for a walk and get some pizza." One of the girls climbs out of the lap she's in and presents Rick with a joint, without so much as a glance at Duney, who feels as if she has somehow turned transparent. As she watches Rick inhale, she imagines hanging the girl by the back of her halter top over a huge tub of strawberry perfume until she begs for mercy. This is the first time Rick has smoked dope in her presence, though she knows he does it, and he knows she knows. She can find no comfortable place to cast her eyes, not on her brother, or on the couples making out on the couch, or on Riggy, gyrating smoothly back and forth on the drum stool. She should not be here; she is an irritating presence. It seems obvious to her that the young girls are the real reason these guys came over, not to listen to Rick's band. It makes her angry to see her brother taken advantage of, but she's not going to say anything; she knows he wouldn't listen if she did. And after all, it's his party.

"I'm going back upstairs," she says.

"Right," says Rick. "See ya."

————

Duney makes her way back to her room and lies on her bed, staring up as she has a thousand times at the sworled patterns in the wood grain of the underside of the upper bunk. There is one spot that looks like an eye, and she remembers thinking once, after coming home from Sunday school, that it was in fact the eye of God, or at least a kind of peephole from which He could look down on her. Now she thinks it looks like a spinning galaxy, or maybe just a large chestnut. She's not sure. From downstairs she hears the sounds of her brother and the others leaving, a lot of indistinct voices echoing in the stairwell, then the slamming of the kitchen door and silence. For a while she listens to the silence, which feels like cotton around her ears. Then she closes her eyes.

When she opens them suddenly, aware of tiny sounds from across the hall, she is unsure if she has been asleep or not. As quietly as she can, she gets up and walks out of her room. There is someone in her parents' bedroom. She looks in and sees it is Riggy.

"What are you doing in here?" she says, surprised at the sharpness of her own voice.

He turns around. He has been sitting on the bed, fooling with the television. "Nothing," he says.

"You're not supposed to be up here. Didn't my brother tell you that? What do you think you're doing?"

"Nothing," he says again. "I just thought I'd watch a little TV. Your brother said to make myself at home."

She takes another step into the room, suspicious. "There's a television downstairs."

"OK, so I was exploring a little. Sorry, I'll split." He looks sincerely apologetic, and Duney wishes she hadn't come on so angry. He also has nice eyes, she notices.

"I thought everybody went out for something to eat."

"They did. I wasn't hungry."

"Well," she says. She can think of nothing else.

"I didn't catch your name," he says, standing. "I'm Riggy."

"Duney."

"Duney? What kind of name is that?"

"Actually, Rick gave it to me. When he was little, he couldn't say 'Diana' right—he was always tagging after me saying 'Duney.' It just stuck."

"Sounds like a cartoon character. 'Duney T. Chucklehound, Private Investigator.' Something like that."

She laughs. "It's better than 'Riggy.' That sounds like a disease."

"Riegert Banks," he says, grinning. "It's a family name. Not many people know it, and I'd appreciate it if you didn't spread it around."

She likes this, the fact that they both have nicknames, though she's tired of her own. She has been planning on dropping it entirely once she leaves for school. "Duney" is no name for a grown woman.

"Even Rick and I aren't allowed in here," she says, taking another step into the room.

"Why not? It's only a room." Riggy has shoulder length brown hair and thick eyebrows that knit together when he speaks. His eyes are bright, bright blue.

"Would you like a drink?" she offers. She is amazed at herself for saying it. She wonders how drunk she really is.

"Hey now, that sounds real good." Where Riggy was sitting on the bed, Duney sees a noticeable depression. She leads him from the room, conscious of his thick, ungainly presence behind her. If he touches anything, she thinks, he'll probably break it.

At the liquor cabinet, he chooses bourbon, and she winces as he pours himself nearly a half glass. Unwilling to make any more obvious inroads, she extracts a dusty bottle of Campari from the back of the cabinet and pours herself an equal amount.

"Ever had that stuff?" he asks.

"Sure, I drink it all the time." In fact, she has no idea what it will taste like, but she is already pleased with the way it looks, like liquid rubies in her glass.

They sit in the living room and sip their drinks. Riggy leans way back in his chair, filling it entirely, crossing his legs with the ease of someone who feels right at home. Even though he must be seven or eight years older than she, Duney likes the fact that he doesn't make a big deal about it.

"Your brother didn't say he had a sister," he says. "Otherwise, I might have come to visit sooner."

"You know he's only fifteen."

Riggy shrugs. "You can do a lot at fifteen. I know I did. Got into all kinds of trouble." He sips at his drink and examines a scuff mark on one of his black leather boots.

"You mean those two teenyboppers downstairs?" she says, teasing. "I'll bet *they* do a lot."

"I wouldn't know about that. I just came along for the ride and to take a look at a guitar. Fifteen isn't my style. I'm not saying there's anything wrong with it though. Just not for me."

"Oh." says Duney, "So what is your style? Forty-year-old divorcees?" She can't believe she is having this conversation. She wishes she had a tape recorder.

"My style," he says, "is something for other people to figure out. I do what I want and let the rest of the world worry about it."

"Just a ramblin' man, huh?"

He looks at her quite seriously. "That's right," he says. "That's exactly it. Hey, don't laugh."

But she can't help it, she is giggling. "I'm sorry," she says, putting a hand over her mouth. "I was thinking about what you must have looked like when you were a little boy. I can picture you walking around everywhere with a set of cap guns on." She can't control her laughter — it spills from her in nervous eruptions. "I'm sorry. I must be drunk."

"Damn," says Riggy.

Taking a deep breath, she manages to stop. The corners of her eyes are wet with tears.

"You want to go for a ride?" asks Riggy.

"A ride?"

"That's right, the Riggy-mobile's right outside."

She feels bad that she has insulted him, and looking around the living room with its neatly vacuumed corners, the carefully hung paintings and photographs, she thinks she wouldn't mind getting out of here at all, for a while. She takes another gulp of the sweet, thick liquid in her glass.

"Absolutely," she says. "Who would I be to pass up the Riggy-mobile?"

———

The interior of Riggy's station wagon smells of gasoline and stale cigarette ash. The dashboard is full of vacancies — there are gaping holes where the glove compartment and radio ought to be. Empty beer bottles collide on the floor of the backseat whenever they make a turn — a dumb, cheerful, clunking sound. Duney is feeling drunk and strangely aggressive. She makes Riggy drive right through the center of town, hoping that someone will see them — one of her friends, or one of her parents' friends even, it doesn't matter. She just likes the idea of being spotted in this beat-up car alongside someone so disreputable. But they see no one she knows, and besides, it is dark out, so even if they did, she would just look like anyone else, out for an evening cruise.

The air has cooled, but it is still extremely humid, and at the far end of town, after Duney has made him drive up and down the main street three times, Riggy pulls up to a stoplight and puts a hand on her knee. "I've got an idea," he says. "Let's go for a swim."

"A swim? Now?"

His hand squeezes momentarily, then returns to the wheel. "At the quarry," he says. "It's about seven miles. What do you say?"

She knows she should not do this, but there is a childishness to Riggy that she finds appealing, and while she doesn't exactly trust him, he doesn't scare her either. She likes the way he seems to know exactly what he wants, unlike the boys her own age she's been out with, who drive her crazy with indecision — where to go for dinner, what movie to see, whose car to take — as if any of that really mattered. She feels she is on an adventure, and to cut it short now might be to cheat herself out of some chance she'll never have again.

"I love to swim," she says.

Just outside of town, Riggy pulls into a small tavern that Duney has never seen before. He leaves the engine running and comes out a few minutes later with a six-pack of beer. Her stomach turns a little as she mentally runs down the list of different drinks she has had since this afternoon. She tries to think of some reason to refuse another, but before she can speak they are moving, and Riggy has placed a freshly opened can into her hands.

"Do you always drink and drive?"

"Always."

She nods, then leans back and kicks her feet up onto the dashboard. "What about your friends? Aren't they going to wonder where you went?"

"I doubt it," he says. "Anyway, we won't be gone long."

She wonders what he means by "I doubt it."

———

There is an access road to the quarry that ends at a locked gate, and they have to leave the car there and climb over. Riggy helps her, putting his hands on her hips and giving her a boost. Then he hands the beers to her and swings himself easily up and over. He tells her they are on private land, and so they keep silent as they walk down the dirt road. Duney's consciousness is at once numbed and heightened. The trees seem to whisper at her as they catch and release the soft, warm breezes. Riggy, who had seemed so clumsy inside the house, walks with powerful, assured strides. He is in his element out here, or at least he acts like it. Duney has to struggle to keep up.

When they get to the quarry, he tells her they can make noise. "No one can hear us out here," he says. "The sound gets trapped." Around them, blasted granite walls rise, crooked and tall. About ten feet below, a large, dark pool of water reflects the newly risen moon.

"I didn't know this was here," she says.

"Most people don't. The ones who do try to keep it a secret." He sits on a ledge and dangles his feet, then opens himself another beer. When he offers one to her, she refuses. She is feeling a little dizzy.

"Come here. Have a seat."

Duney does so. The odd, shadowy lighting of the place makes her feel as if she is in a movie.

Before she even realizes it is happening, Riggy is kissing her. For a moment, she lets him, but then she pulls away. "Hey," she says.

"Hey what?"

"Hey cut that out. I'm not some fifteen-year-old groupie. I thought we came out here for a swim." She is suddenly aware of the vulnerability of her situation. She thinks about Beth Ann telling her to watch out, and how she has done exactly the opposite.

"Sure, we came out here to swim." He leans over to kiss her again, and again she pulls away. "What's the matter?" he says.

"I don't know about this."

He laughs, stands, and begins unbuttoning his shirt. "It's dark, and there's no one going to see you anyway." He continues to strip until he is down to his underwear, a baggy pair of boxer shorts. Duney stares out over the water, pretending not to watch, but stealing glances at him every now and then. He has a strong, mus- cled body with an extremely hairy chest and legs. He also has a potbelly, probably from drinking so much beer, and she sees him suck it in to make it less noticeable. There is something incredibly normal about this; she wishes her brother were here to see that guitar players grow older like anyone else. Somewhere below them, a rock drips water slowly into the pool, a quiet, monotonous sound.

"Well? Are you just going to sit there or what?"

Standing, she begins to undress, and as she removes each garment, she becomes more and more nervous. When she is down to her underwear, she turns her back to him, feeling tiny and foolish. She wishes she were still at home.

"Come on," says Riggy, "Don't give me this. I didn't drag you here, you wanted to come. Let's have some fun. I'll go first." He leans forward and dives into the black water. For a moment, Duney is gratefully alone on the ledge. Then he emerges a few yards away, tossing his long hair like a wet dog, blowing water out of his mouth. "It's great!" he shouts.

There is a horrible inevitability to all of this, Duney thinks, as hard and unrelenting as the rock ledge beneath her feet. She thinks of Riggy sitting on her parents' bed and wonders if he might not have been planning to steal the television, rather than watch it. Until she came along and gave him something better to do. It seems entirely possible, but she realizes she'll never know, and she's not sure that it matters really, or that she cares. She slips a finger under her bra strap and pulls it up on her shoulder, then, taking a deep breath, dives in. The water is icy cold and has a hard, mineral cleanness to it. When she comes up, Riggy is next to her. He puts a hand out underwater and touches her.

She splashes water at him and begins to swim away. He starts out after her, and suddenly she is seized by an awful fear, and she swims as hard as she can. She is going to be raped, she thinks, possibly murdered, her body never found out here in this lonely place, and it will be her own fault. Riggy splashes and kicks furiously, but for all his output of energy, he is an inefficient swimmer, and she finds it easy to pull away. Relieved, she allows herself to enjoy the cold smoothness of the water. From the opposite end of the pool he shouts that he will catch her, and she lets him get close before pushing off and moving effortlessly away from him once again. When she has put the distance of the whole pool between them, she does a lazy back stroke. She thinks she has never felt more in control in her life, and she almost wishes it could go on forever, this easy gliding back and forth. The water supports her, caresses her, is in league with all her movements. From the other side, Riggy takes a deep breath and prepares another assault. When he is halfway across, she pushes off, dodges him in the middle, then easily swims past in the other direction.

She begins to circle the edges of the pool, taking long, powerful strokes, aware all the time of Riggy's clumsy pursuit. She feels if she wanted to, she could just go on and on and never get tired, that Riggy might drown himself in his own desire and she'd still be going around in circles, even as the sun came up. Behind her, Riggy is shouting something, and she lifts her head out of the water to listen. "Diana," he yells, "Diana." Bouncing off the rock walls, his voice seems to come from everywhere at once, even from inside her own head. Taking a deep breath, she continues to swim, but she slows her pace, just enough.

# EL DIABLO DE LA CIENEGA

The black sports car that pulled up in a puff of dust alongside the La Cienega Community Center looked like a big hand, placed palm down in the red dirt. Ignoring it, Victor kept his feet in front of the chalked line on the cracked concrete. The door clicked open and a very tanned man with straw-colored hair got out, stuck his hands into the pockets of his chinos, and leaned back to watch. No time left on the clock, Spurs down by one. As always, the game had come down to this one deciding moment. Victor made the first shot, then lobbed up the second for the win. There had never really been any doubt. Just for the hell of it, he made them again.

The late afternoon sun glinted off the broken windshields of a half-dozen wrecked and rusting cars across the road. Beyond them sat nine mobile homes, all in poor repair, set at odd angles to each other. The community center, a square building with flaking yellow stucco and one intact window, sported a tiny sign indicating that it had also once served as the La Cienega Volunteer Fire Department. From the south wall, a faded outline of a mural of the Virgin someone had begun long ago and never finished gazed out, faceless. The building was abandoned but, with the exception of a few weedy cracks in its surface, the basketball court alongside it was still in good shape.

Victor looked over briefly at the man, then continued shooting. He tossed in seven consecutive baskets before one finally circled the rim and hopped back out.

"Hope I didn't make you nervous," called the man.

Victor, twelve, had recently experienced a growth spurt that had turned him into a gangly, stretched-out cartoon of what he'd looked like the year before. He was particularly sensitive to criticism. Catching the ball, he responded by spinning around and executing a perfect hook shot that touched nothing but net. He turned and faced the man.

"Victor Garcia?"

"Sure," said Victor.

"I've heard about you." The man got up from where he was leaning and walked onto the court. He wore a pink LaCoste shirt and Top-Siders. The license plate on his car said Texas. "I like to shoot a little hoop myself now and then. Usually, when I go someplace new, I ask around to find out who's good."

Victor eyed him with suspicion, but also a certain amount of pride. It was, after all, about time he got some attention.

"Fact."

"Who'd you ask?"

He waved his hand in the general direction from which he'd come. "Guy up the road."

"Lopez?"

"I think he said his name was Lopez. What's the difference? He was right. You've got the touch. Not everybody does, you know. Just the right balance of things—you concentrate well, but you're relaxed, too."

Victor glanced across the street, where a tiny dust devil spun in the yard in front of Rodriguez's place. "What are you, CIA?" he asked.

The man shook his head and chuckled. "Close, though. FOA. Ferrari Owners of America."

"Ferrari? That's what this is?"

The man smiled, his lips drawing back to reveal a set of china-white teeth, and waved toward his car. "You have to pass a stupidity test to qualify for one. Getting parts is murder. On my fourth clutch. I'm up here for a convention. Southwest chapter — we're meeting in Santa Fe this year. I always try to drive around and see the country a little. It's beautiful out here — all these extinct volcanoes. Kind of violent, if you know what I mean. You're lucky to live where you do."

"I guess," Victor said, dubiously. He didn't feel particularly lucky.

"I mean it. Look around. It's true what they say about northern New Mexico. There's a quality to the light. Sky's as blue as a polished gemstone. What do you all say? 'The Land of Enchantment?'" He raised his hands as if demonstrating a magic trick, then smiled and indicated that Victor should give him the ball, which he did. He bounced it once, then took a shot — a perfect swish. The hairs on his muscled arms stood high off the skin, making him appear to have a kind of golden aura. Victor retrieved the ball.

"Nice," he said, passing it back. Phony as blue macaroni, he thought to himself, which was something Rodriguez liked to say. A hunk of old metal tubing lay on the ground a few feet away, and Victor figured if he needed, he could probably get to it quick enough to inflict some damage.

The stranger eyed the basket and did it again.

"Victor Garcia," he said, walking over to get the ball from the pile of rubble where it had rolled. "Are you a betting man?"

"I got nothing to bet," Victor said.

"That's OK. We can negotiate. I just think it might be fun to have a little competition — you and me. Friendly."

He decided the stranger was harmless. "Free throws?"

"Maybe. Maybe something a little more challenging."

A car came up the road, its muffler dragging noisily on the dirt and gravel. Victor's mother was returning home from the motel where she changed sheets.

"I got to go," Victor said, taking back his ball, though reluctantly. He would have liked to show this man what he could do.

From his pocket, the man withdrew a black leather wallet, and out of that he took a business card which he handed to Victor. It read: E. Crispin Light, Import/Export.

"Most of my friends just call me Money," he said. "It's my basketball name."

"Money?"

"You know — money in the bank. Kind of like Bill Bradley was 'Dollar Bill.' "

Victor looked again at the card. The printing on it was in gold. "What does the *E* stand for?"

"Good, good," said Money, grinning. "Most people don't even ask. The fact is, it doesn't stand for anything. I put it on there because I think it looks classy. What do you think?"

Victor shrugged. Across the road, he could see his mom struggling with groceries. "You coming back?"

"You bet." Money looked at his watch. "Tomorrow evening. Will you be here?"

"I'm always here," said Victor, coolly.

"All right. You go on home now and look after your mom."

Victor shielded his eyes against a sudden gust of wind that threw a curtain of dust up around them. "What do you know about my mom?"

"Did I say I knew anything?" He smiled. "I'll see you tomorrow, Victor." He shook the boy's hand. His was hard and calloused as if, even though he appeared to be rich, he still did a fair amount of manual labor. Gardening, maybe, Victor thought. The man got back into his car and drove off in the direction of the setting sun.

————

The understanding came to him clearly, in the middle of the night, when he awoke to the sound of his mother's coughing. This was a nightly occurrence — the luminous readout on his alarm clock said 3:06, and as he lay waiting for the sounds to subside, he was filled with a mixture of fear and pride. He really was good. Not just good the way anyone who practices enough can become good, but special.

He got up and went into the kitchen to make himself a cocktail, his name for the milk, Nestle's Quik and raw egg drink he'd invented as part of his personal training regimen. From her bedroom, his mother continued to cough, a deep, body-racking sound that seemed to originate in her stomach and work its way up.

Taking his drink, he unlocked the door and stepped outside. There were stars everywhere, more than he'd ever seen. In the darkness, the shapes of the wrecked cars were ominous, lurking monsters. Victor walked toward them, if only to prove to himself he wasn't scared. Something moved on one of the hoods and he halted. Gradually, his eyes became more accustomed to the light and he saw a small lizard. It was watching him.

"It's you, isn't it?" he said.

The lizard did not move. Even out here, the sound of his mother's hacking was clearly audible, the only disturbance in the night's solemn quiet.

"I'm ready to deal," said Victor. "I know who you are. I know what you want. I'm not afraid. If I lose, you can have my soul, to be damned to eternal hellfire. But if I win, I want you to make my mom OK again." He paused for a moment, considering whether to throw in something else, too, like a million dollars, or a starting position with the San Antonio Spurs, but it seemed to him that if he were fighting the forces of darkness, it would be best to keep his own motives as pure and true as possible. "Tomorrow," he said. "Sundown."

The lizard continued to look at him. Then, to Victor's astonishment, it nodded its head once and scurried away.

As he passed his mother's door on his way back to bed, Victor stopped and whispered, "It's all right. I'm taking care of everything."

——

But E. Crispin Light did not appear the next evening. Victor spent over two hours on the basketball court, dribbling, shooting, working on the basics, keeping his eye out for the black sports car. It was too bad, because his shooting was dead accurate — he hit nineteen out of twenty from the free throw line. He felt certain he could have beaten all comers, even an emissary from the Prince of Darkness. Eventually, as the light began to fade, he put his ball under one arm and walked home.

His mother was watching *Wheel of Fortune*.

"If only I could spell a little better," she lamented. "I'd go to Hollywood and clean up on this game." She held a small clay pot in one hand, a paintbrush in the other. She picked up extra money painting Anasazi designs onto local pottery for sale to tourists. She was very pale. Victor's father had been Mexican, but his mother was from California, a thin woman of Irish extraction, with large, sad eyes. Though she'd been sick now on and off for the better part of a year, she refused to go to a doctor. They had no insurance. Her one gesture toward her health had been to quit smoking, but it had only seemed to make the coughing worse. She held out a pot. "Want to try one?"

Victor shook his head. "I'm thinking," he said.

"What you need is some friends," she said. "You spend too much time alone."

"I don't need no friends," he said.

"Any. 'I don't need any friends.'" She raised her eyebrows, then drew a line around the lip of the vase. "Alabaster caught a lizard this morning. Tore the poor thing to bits."

Victor swallowed hard. "A lizard?"

"You know. One of those grayish ones."

Alabaster, who was part Persian, lay in the windowsill, cleaning her paws. Victor stared at her, trying to see if she looked any different. After all, he reasoned, it might have been any lizard.

"Are you all right?" asked his mother. "You look a little pale."

"I'm fine," he said. "How are you?"

"Oh, on a scale of one to ten, today was about a four, I'd say."

"It's going to get better," he told her. Then he excused himself and went to his room.

———

The plaza in Santa Fe was filled with Ferraris, all of them polished to a radiance, reflecting sunlight, smelling richly of gasoline
and leather. They were arranged by year and model — scores of
them parked side to side, their owners hovering about, keeping a
wary eye out for people who might ignore the "Do Not Touch"
signs in their windshields. Victor locked his bicycle and wandered
among the automobiles, looking for one in particular. After making almost a complete circuit of the plaza, he found it, wedged in
among six others of exactly the same style, but the only black one
with Texas plates. He looked around for Money, but he was not in
the immediate area. Victor peered in, cupping his hands to the
tinted glass, half-expecting to see a dance of writhing, tortured
souls. The inside did look like another world, but only a wealthy
one. The control panel was polished walnut, the seats a deep, red
leather. There was a Willie Nelson cassette in the tape deck,
a New Mexico highway map on the dashboard. A little disap-
pointed, he stuck his hands in his pockets and turned.

"Hello, Victor." For a Texan, Money had almost no accent at
all. He wore sunglasses and a maroon golf shirt.

"What happened?" said Victor. "You didn't come."

"Yeah, sorry about that. We had a big dinner at the hotel and it
got late. I'll make it up to you."

Victor tried to seem as though he didn't care. "You're the one
wanted to come and shoot."

"I realize that, and I feel badly about it. If I'd had your number, I
would have called."

Victor didn't mention that for the past two months, as a part of
an economizing measure, they'd been doing without a phone. He
thought again of the lizard. "You were where?"

"At a dinner. That's what we do at these conventions. We drive
our cars to some central location, then hang around eating and
drinking. It's pretty boring, really, but it gets me out of the office.
Buy you an ice cream?"

Victor accepted, and the two of them took their cones to a
bench.

Money took off his glasses. "Have you decided what you want
to play for?"

Victor met his eyes, which seemed to him like cold, blue stones. He thought of the devil movies he'd seen. It seemed a peculiar question. "Do I have a choice?"

"There's always a choice. Only remember, never get into a bet you're not prepared to lose."

"I'm not going to lose. And you're going to help my mother."

"What are you suggesting, Victor?"

"She can't sleep, and she's got trouble with her breathing."

"Then she ought to see a doctor."

"Give her back her health," said Victor. "If I win, that's what I want."

He took out a set of black driving gloves and swatted a fly that had landed on his knee. "And if I win?"

"You can have my soul."

Money arched an eyebrow. "Your soul?"

Victor nodded. "You heard me."

"Big stakes."

"Yes."

Money thought this over for a moment. He bit into the cone part of his ice cream and chewed noisily, then swallowed. "I think you may have mistaken me for someone else. I'm only a business-man who likes to play a little ball. But all right, you're on."

Just then, a man with a bullhorn made an announcement.

"That's my category," said Money. "Let's go see if I won any-thing."

Victor followed him to where a man in a plaid jacket stood next to a blonde lady in a white jumpsuit, carrying a clipboard. She took the bullhorn and announced the winner's name, and a fat man in a brown cowboy hat jumped up to accept the plaque.

Victor watched Money's reaction, expecting to see anger, pos-sibly rage. The potential seemed there — behind Money's cool, sculpted face, there was a hint of something smoldering, competi-tive and mean. But he just shook his head.

"These things are all fixed," he said. "I don't even know why I bother."

———

The evening was a hot one, with only the vaguest hint of a breeze from the southwest. Victor was out on the court early, dribbling around, working on his bank shot. True to his word, Money appeared a little after seven, his black car still shiny as glass in spite of the dust its tires kicked up. The engine roared and was silent.

He was dressed in worn blue gym shorts and a red tank top, and his sneakers were red canvas high-tops from another era. He was muscled and trim, but he looked very human, and for a minute, Victor wondered if he might be wrong about him. Maybe he really was what he claimed, just a rich guy who liked to play basketball. But the devil could be a trickster—he knew that from Rodriguez's woman, Opal, whose entire life seemed to be made up of encounters with him. The Evil One took a special interest, she said, in tormenting her. Just last week, a mysterious wind had taken a sheet off her clothesline and hung it from the branches of a nearby cottonwood, where it flapped like a sail for two days because Opal refused to have anything to do with it. She'd finally given Victor fifty cents to climb up and get it.

Money tossed a basketball to Victor, who caught it and examined its material and make. Leather, with no visible trademark—good grain, easy to grip. He bounced it and took a set shot which fell two feet short of the basket. He adjusted and proceeded to put the next five into the net. "I'm ready," he said.

"We'll play Death," said Money. "A game of accuracy. Shoot to go first."

"Don't you want to warm up?"

"I'm always warm. Go ahead."

Victor took a foul shot and sank it. Then Money went to the line, crouched with the ball under his chin, eyed the basket and shot. The ball bounced off the rim.

Victor grinned. "Maybe you should have warmed up."

"Your shot," said Money.

Victor figured he'd go for it, right from the start. He walked off the court, over to where the Ferrari was parked, and from there put up a long, high, arching shot. It looped three times around the rim and flew out.

"Don't be too cocky," said Money. "Rule number one." He collected the ball, dribbled out to a crack in the pavement where the top of the key would have been and executed a turnaround jumper that fell perfectly through the hole.

Victor took the ball and repeated the shot. Still, he was furious with himself for giving up the advantage. Now, he was on the defensive, forced to wait for his opponent to miss.

Shot for shot, they were both perfect. Money did a backward lay-up, but Victor easily made one too. Fall-away jumpers, hook shots, they each sank everything they put up. Finally, after nearly five minutes, a sloppy jump shot gave the advantage back to Victor. He put in a twenty-foot banker. Money whistled, walked to the spot and did the same. Rather than try something else, Victor took the shot again — he had a sense that he'd make it, and he figured he'd keep going from the same place until Money missed. He didn't have to wait. Money's attempt went off the backboard, missing the rim entirely.

"You've got *D*," said Victor, a little louder than he'd intended.

"Just shoot the ball," said Money.

————

It went on, a slow game, a game of nerves and of strategy. Money kept trying to distract him.

"Are you worried? I know I would be. You've got a lot at stake here."

"I'm not scared," said Victor. In fact, he was getting a little nervous. He'd never thought the contest would last this long.

"But your soul. That's a big wager. Maybe you're betting over your head."

"You don't scare me."

"I'm not trying to scare you. I'm trying to let you know that I appreciate the seriousness of your convictions. For me, basketball has always just been a game. I don't let it obsess me the way you do. That's why I'm going to win, because I have less at stake. I'm more relaxed."

"If it was just a game to you, how come you came out here to find me?" Victor went to the foul line, stood with his back to the basket, and put the ball in backward, over his head.

"Well," said Money, "isn't that special?" He tried the shot and missed.

"*D-E* for you," said Victor.

————

Within a few minutes, Victor started missing shots, ones he should have been making. Money played with an icy calm, calculating his shots like geometry problems. It was as if, Victor thought, unseen forces were acting upon him, making him miss. To make matters worse, each time he did, Money smiled at him and said "thunk." Pretty soon, Victor was behind, with three letters. Glancing over at the Ferrari, he saw that Alabaster was curled up on the hood, sunning herself. It was, he thought, a very bad sign.

"We can quit now," said Money. "I don't mind."

"No way."

"Don't kid yourself, Victor. You're going to lose, in spite of that name of yours. But it doesn't matter. There's nothing magical about being a good basketball player. It won't do anything for you down the road, other than make you wish you spent your time on something more useful. You'll never be a great — you've got no killer instinct. And you're too short."

"Stop talking," said Victor.

"Just trying to get you to be realistic."

Just then, one of Rodriguez's dogs got loose, ran across the street, and began barking at the stranger. Money froze in the middle of the court as the black-and-white mongrel bared her teeth and snarled, tail flat down as if she expected at any moment to be kicked. Rodriguez himself appeared after about a minute, a beer in his hand, to grab the dog by the collar.

"Who's winning?" he asked.

"That's one fierce hound," said Money, nervously keeping his distance. "Hunter?"

"No hunter," said Rodriguez. "She's a lover. Just had her third litter this year." He pursed his lips, eyeing this stranger with the nice car. "You want some puppies?"

"No, thanks," said Money.

"Ten bucks," said Rodriguez. He was a squat, muscular man, with a hank of hair that dangled loosely over his forehead.

"I don't much like dogs."

"No, man. Ten bucks the kid beats you."

"Well. Ten bucks it is," said Money. "Where were we?"

"My shot," said Victor. Think no bad thoughts, he told himself. Keep your heart pure. He put in a running hook.

Money made his hook, picked up his own rebound, and bounced the ball back to Victor.

"I need another beer," announced Rodriguez, and dragged the dog back across the street. He returned moments later with a six-pack and settled in the dirt by the side of the court to watch. After a little while, he was joined by Opal, her heavyset, Navajo features almost making it seem as if she were wearing a mask. She broke open one of the beers and tipped her head back to receive the contents.

Over by the trailers, the competition across the road was attracting attention. Many of the residents began to emerge to see what was going on. The two long-hair drunks whom everyone called Manny and Moe, and who worked as part-time construction workers when they weren't sleeping off the booze, walked slow circles around Money's car, nodding their heads and making approving comments. Distracted by them, or maybe just growing tired, Money bounced one off the rim.

"That's *D-E-A*," said Rodriguez, who had appointed himself referee.

"I know what it is," said Money. "Please, don't touch the car."

There was now a small crowd gathered — nearly fifteen people. Somebody brought out potato chips and passed them around. Victor felt as if he were in a spotlight. These were people who generally ignored each other, except for a nod in passing, but there was a real sense of community as they watched the contest. Last to come out was Victor's mother. Shielding her eyes against the slanted light, she looked pale and ghostlike. The wind, which was beginning to pick up as it always did at this time of day, tossed her housedress around her knees.

Victor did a reverse lay-up. There was a smattering of applause.

The sweat stood out on Money's face as he bounced the ball in preparation. Then he moved under the basket and flipped the ball backward over his head. As he did so, one ankle buckled and he went tumbling forward onto the pavement.

"Damn," he said, holding the ankle in front of him like a foreign object. He kneaded it for a few moments, then hobbled to his feet.

"*D-E-A-T*," sang Rodriguez. "Uh-oh."

Victor considered. Repeating the lay-up would finish Money off easily — with his twisted ankle, he wouldn't have a chance. But it seemed like a cheap ending, and Victor had an audience. He wanted to do something spectacular.

"Everything on this shot," he heard himself say.

"Everything?" Money said, cautiously. "Are you sure?"

"Everything."

"Done," said Money.

"What are you guys playing for, anyway?" asked Rodriguez. When there was no answer, he shrugged and opened another beer.

Victor walked the ball right off the court, out into the dirt lot beyond it, a few feet from a particularly nasty-looking cholla. The crowd let out a cheerful noise, encouraging, but with laughter mixed in — no one believed for a moment that the wiry, sad-faced twelve year old could possibly hurl a ball that far, let alone make it go through a hoop. Money hobbled around in obvious pain, but the look of amusement on his face was unmistakable.

Victor knew the moment he looked at the basket and saw how far he was away, that this was impossible. He'd overdone it — he was way beyond his range. But he couldn't see any way out now without losing face. In his hands the ball seemed to gain weight, as if it were filling internally with liquid. Money was still smiling at him. His neighbors watched in anticipation. His mother stood among them, her hands clenched in fists at her sides. He'd blown it, he told himself. He'd failed to stay pure. Pride was one of the seven deadly sins (he was pretty sure about this), and his own had brought him to the brink of the abyss.

Holding the ball to his chest, he gauged the distance to the net and prayed for a miracle. He did not want to die. He tried to imagine what it would be like to spend eternity soulless, in a box, no air, no light, the rough wood pressed up against his face. For a moment, he felt as if his feet had grown roots and that his bones extended deep down into the earth, into places damp, fungal, and cool. Then he put the ball as high into the air as he could possibly throw it.

Moving in what seemed like slow motion, the ball described an orange-brown arc, at the very top of which it hung for a moment, certain to fall short. Then, out of the south, a powerful wind kicked up, and for a moment, the whole world seemed to shake. Tumbleweed rolled around the court, and the rim of Rodriguez's beer can was coated with red-brown dust. Descending on the shoulders of the wind, the ball actually cleared the basket, arriving first at the backboard, then glancing smoothly down through the net.

Victor screamed at the top of his lungs, and his voice was joined by a chorus of others from across the road.

"Never happen again in a million years," said Rodriguez, walking onto the court.

"Lucky," said Money, shaking his head.

"Hey, man," said Rodriguez. "He beat you square and fair. Pay up."

Money hobbled over to his car and brought back a wallet. He took out a ten and gave it to Rodriguez.

"You don't owe the kid no cash?" asked Rodriguez.

"No," said Money. "I don't."

"So, what then?"

Money shrugged and shook Victor's hand, then went back to his car and got in.

"What about our deal?" said Victor. He felt suddenly anxious, more so than he had during the game.

Money leaned his head out the window and looked at him long and hard. "I never expected to lose," he said at last. His tinted window hummed and closed, leaving Victor staring at his own reflection. Then the Ferrari's engine fired, coughing dust out around the back tires. Spewing gravel behind him, Money pulled out onto the street and headed in the direction of the county road.

"Fucking Texans," said Rodriguez. "Think they own the

world." He spat into the dirt. "You shoot pretty good basketball, my friend. But you don't know the first thing about gambling." He turned and headed back, Opal following at his heels. Across the street, most of the onlookers had already returned to their trailers.

Victor's mother put a hand on his head. "Did you bet with that man?" she asked.

Victor said nothing.

"What did you bet?"

He didn't answer. The wind that had come and carried his shot home was gone, and in its place, the evening crept in, cool and still.

She shook her head in frustration. "I don't know what it is with you these days," she said. "I don't know what you're thinking." She put her forehead up against his and stared directly into his eyes, but he was silent. "Don't stay out too long," she told him finally. She walked back across the street.

Alone now on the court, Victor saw that Money had left his ball. It sat in the dirt, near where his car had been parked. He picked it up and bounced it a few times, the smack it made against the concrete seeming to echo off the surrounding hills, a lonely, casual sound. He felt cheated. Still, something had happened — he knew that. He would not allow himself the easy luxury of disappointment. For a brief moment, the powers of the universe had convened in his fingertips. He watched the lights come on in the different trailers, listened to the sounds of Opal and Rodriguez starting up one of their nightly arguments. He bounced the ball a few more times in the dimming light, watching his shadow move against the pavement, taller than any man's and growing longer with each passing minute.

# TAXES

retzel and Ronnie stand on the corner in front of the deserted Shabazz Steak and Take, huddled back a little to take advantage of a slight overhang of the roof and stay out of the rain. Ronnie, lean and muscular, his hair cut into a flattop, hunkers down, cups his hands, and lights another Newport. Pretzel is smaller, skinnier, and does not smoke. It isn't his health that concerns him, just the waste of money.

"You set up, man," says Ronnie.

"Forget it," says Pretzel. "Just forget it." Across the street, behind stained plate-glass windows, a shadowy figure moves slowly back and forth. The cracked plastic sign overhead reads simply "Tax."

"Chump change. Nickels and dimes. That's all you ever going to get out of him." Ronnie puts the toe of his sneaker into a puddle, testing its depth.

"Bought me this coat." A cheap blue parka with a fake fur-lined hood hangs on Pretzel's narrow frame, the nylon material shining off and on in the reflected light from passing cars.

"Ugly," says Ronnie, breathing smoke. "I wouldn't never wear no coat like that." Ronnie's coat is silver colored sheepskin, but Pretzel knows how he got it.

"How much you carry last night?"

"I don't know."

"Come on, man."

"Eleven hundred."

Ronnie whistles. "Damn."

Pretzel watches the cigarette ember grow brighter as Ronnie sucks on it. "Forget it." He checks his watch. "I got to go over now. Where you staying?"

"With my lady." He throws the butt into a puddle where it hisses and dies. "Think it over. He don't care about you." He pulls his collar up around his neck, shoves his hands deep into his pockets, and steps out into the rain.

————

Fishman does not look up when Pretzel comes in, just tells him to lock the door. The tax man's feet ache — they seem to have swollen two sizes inside his battered loafers — and he wishes he were home where he could take them out, put them up on the table, read the paper. Out of the corner of his eye he watches the boy perch on one of the torn chairs, shake a few drops of rain off his head. Fishman inscribes numbers in his ledger book, adds daily totals, compares those figures to last year's, estimates what percentage of his total business has already pushed its way through the heavy glass doors. Every year Fishman raises his prices 10 percent, and every year business drops off by not quite that number. He feels a detached, almost scientific curiosity about the trend.

"Just a couple of minutes, Pretz," he says, punching up some numbers on his calculator. "Big day today."

It is seven o'clock, closing time, and Pretzel is always punctual. Sometimes, if a client comes in at the last moment, Fishman will make him wait until he takes their information. Though he wears a watch — an ugly, multifunction thing his older son bought him seven years ago as a wedding present — he rarely looks at it. He depends instead on Pretzel.

While he waits, Pretzel walks around the office and checks out the supplies, which it is his job to replace. There are still paper cups by the coffee machine, though there is next to no coffee. Still a roll of toilet paper in the bathroom. The cracked linoleum floor is filthy and streaked from the constant in and out of muddy shoes, but he knows Fishman will tell him to wait on that, since the floor is a once a week job, reserved for Sundays when the office is closed. Pretzel gets ten dollars for the floor. Fishman lives in Queens, but still drives in to Brooklyn Sunday mornings, closes the heavy, motorized iron gates around the windows and, sealed off this way, catches up on paperwork. Sundays, Pretzel walks his mother to church, then comes down and bangs three times on the metal so Fishman will know it is him. Then he comes in and mops.

Fishman has been on this same corner now twenty-five years. In that time nearly all the other legitimate businesses have closed down, giving way to smoke shops, numbers spots, simple abandonment and vandalism. He and Eps, who owns the pharmacy across the street, are phantom images of what was once a neighborhood. Now, groups of drunken men gather endlessly on the street corners, and junkies stand shaking in doorways. Fishman dares only walk from his car to his office door, and even this he does in a hurry. He has Pretzel to do what little shopping is necessary, keep the place clean, and every evening after closing, get the money orders from Eps. The way Fishman figures it, crossing the street himself with that kind of cash would be asking for trouble.

"Right," he says, closing the book. "Ready?"

Pretzel nods and stands up.

"Nasty out tonight?"

"Not so bad." He watches the old man's hands as they slip a rubber-banded stack of bills into an envelope.

"How's that coat working out?"

"Warm, Mister F."

"Good, good," he says, without looking at him. "OK, we've got twelve here. Not a bad day, right?" He grins at Pretzel, taking him into his confidence with this information. It is a game they play, pretending that Pretzel is somehow an integral part of the business, and that these daily totals are the result of teamwork.

"Sounds good to me."

"Sounds good to you, huh? All right then, hurry up." He hands Pretzel the envelope, keeping it low in case anyone might be watching. Pretzel sticks it into his pocket, zips up, and steps out into the night.

When he sees who it is, Eps unlocks his door, then locks it again after Pretzel, damp with rain, steps inside. Pretzel feels a kind of odd bond with Eps, if only because he, like Fishman, is an elderly Jewish man in a neighborhood others like him have long since abandoned. But they almost never say anything to each other. Fishman schmoozes with his clients, but Eps is a quiet man, guarding his words as carefully as the dollars he locks up nightly in his safe. He nods at the envelope and steps behind the cash register, where he makes out the money orders: two for five hundred each, one for two hundred. While he waits, Pretzel walks up and down the aisles, examining the medications. He doesn't think Eps likes him much. Still, once years ago when he wasn't feeling well, he gave him some laxative to take home, no charge.

When Eps is through, he peers through his glasses at Pretzel. "I guess you'll be wanting something else to do soon," he says.

Pretzel puts down the bottle of vitamins he has been looking at. "What?"

"I heard Fishman's closing up after this season. I don't blame him. Neighborhood's dead anyway."

"We're doing good business," says Pretzel.

Eps hands him the money orders. "I don't know, it's just what I heard. Anyway, if you need to pick up a couple bucks after he's gone, you come by. I'll find you something."

Crossing back over the street, Pretzel can't believe it. He's been working for Fishman ever since he was little, hanging out in front of the supermarket, making quarters helping people carry their bags home. One day, Fishman stuck his head out of the door and whistled him over because a client had spilled coffee all over the floor, and he needed paper towels. He gave him two dollars and said to get himself something with the change. Along with the towels, he bought a bag of pretzels, which he ate sitting in the chair in front of Fishman's desk. That was seven years ago.

When he returns with the money orders, Fishman is just closing up his briefcase. He takes them and slips them into his pocket.

"Mister F.," says Pretzel, "Eps says you're going to close down."

Fishman smiles. His skin is still rosy from the two weeks he spent in Florida over Christmas. He has a house, two cars, a son who's married and another in medical school. Pretzel suddenly wonders why he has bothered to keep the business open even this long.

"Eps said that?"

"Said come see him if I need work."

"He did, did he?" He picks up his briefcase. "Come on, let's get out of here. Lillian's going to kill me if I'm late again."

Pretzel has never met Fishman's wife, but he knows she is younger than he, and imagines her as very beautiful. She and Fishman play tennis together. "Are you?" he asks.

"I've got a good business here, Pretz. You don't just walk away from a good thing."

After they lower and padlock the gates, Pretzel escorts him to his car, aware that he has not really answered the question. Big Larry, drunk as usual, is seated on the hood, a pint of Popov in his hand, another sticking out of the pocket of his coat. His fly is open, and one knee of his pants is wet, as if he has recently knelt in a puddle. "Professor," he says when he sees them.

"Come on Larry, off the car," says Pretzel.

Larry waves the bottle in the air in front of him. "Oh, you a big man," he says. "A big man."

"Now, Larry."

He heaves himself to the sidewalk, points a finger at Fishman. "I'm a lawyer, man," he says. "I got thousands. Thousands."

"Sure you do," says Pretzel. Fishman unlocks the door and gets in.

"Got me a Cadillac," says Larry.

From inside the car, Fishman waves to Pretzel, then pulls out into the traffic.

"Hey, boy," says Larry, "I seen your brother."

Pretzel looks up at the man's eyes. They are glazed with alcohol, like small plastic buttons. He was probably once an intelligent man, but drink has rotted his brain and made a fool out of him.

"So what?" he says.

Larry shakes his head. "You watch yourself now."

———

Ronnie is waiting for Pretzel outside his house, jaw clenched, eyes yellow and distant. "I need ten bucks," he says.

"And I ain't got it."

"Come on, man, just ten is all. I'll get it back to you tomorrow."

Pretzel digs into his pocket and pulls out a five. "Here, you'll have to get the other five somewheres else."

Ronnie takes the bill from him. "There's more where that came from."

"I told you, forget it."

Ronnie spits. "You protecting a leech. A bloodsucker."

"You ought to know."

"You ought to know I'm right."

"He don't have to stay open — he's got money. People got to do tax." The curtains on the cracked window pull aside and Pretzel can see his mother's round face through the glass, but just for a moment. The curtains fall quickly back into place. "You want to come in?" he asks.

"Right," says Ronnie, then starts to walk away. "You think about it. Do something for yourself for a change."

"Leave off me, man."

"You know I can't do that. I'm your people. Me, not him. It's gonna be you and me long after tax man's gone."

Pretzel watches him leave, then climbs the stairs, one at a time.

———

When he first started, the whole thing had seemed beautifully mysterious. You filled out a blue sheet of paper, sent it in, and the government sent you money. Taxes were a magic trick, and Fishman was the magician. Pretzel would sit for hours watching the people parade in and out: the men in their work boots, the women who, even in the heart of Bed-Stuy, somehow felt it necessary to dress up for the occasion. Teenagers coming to file for the first time, proud of their first job. Occasionally, someone got mad because they felt they were being cheated out of a bigger refund, or they owed. Fishman would calm them with that smooth, knowing voice that said, I understand, I'm on your side. Most of the clients thought Fishman was a gift from God — a man whose hands could turn paper into gold.

They all knew Pretzel, those customers who came back year after year. They'd bring him presents — a cheap hat, some free-sample cologne. Over the years Pretzel had become as much a part of the office as the old, steel-topped desks and the clumsy adding machines used by the preparers Fishman hired for the season. But he was almost done with school now, and already the summer stretched out before him, impossibly long and hot. And beyond that, the rest of his life.

He had a collection of advertisements he'd cut out of the *Post*, and taken from displays on the subway, for different technical schools. He kept them in the center of an old dictionary under the letter *t*. With each one he had been, at least for a while, convinced that he had found his future. Most recently it was Computer Technician, which the Apex Institute promised to teach in one intensive year. He'd brought the ad in to the office and asked Fishman if he knew anything about computers.

"I've got no use for them," he'd said.

"It's a fast-growing field, though," Pretzel quoted the copy. "Lots of earning potential."

"That may be. Is this leading up to something?"

Taking the ad from his pocket, he put it on the desk in front of Fishman, who picked it up and read it over, nodding his head as if it were a legal document and not a three-by-five card. "Did you get this on the subway?" he asked.

Pretzel nodded.

"Well, I'm not going to say it's a bad idea. But you know what I think, right? I think you should forget about these schemes and take control of your life. Transcend, Pretz, transcend. Go to City College and study accounting, or computers even if that's what you want. These Apex Institutes, they're just someone else's get-rich-quick scheme. They're not for you. You know what I'm saying?"

"I think so," said Pretzel.

"I'm saying you don't sit around waiting for something good to happen to you. There are no magic cards waiting for you on the subway, or anywhere else. There's only good, hard work. Nothing comes without a price."

Afterward, Pretzel would reconsider his plans. But always, he saved the ad, slipping it into the hiding place in his dictionary, just in case. He drew comfort from them, as if their very presence guaranteed him options to fall back on. It was easy for Fishman to say make something of yourself. Pretzel knew that transcend meant to rise above. But most of the time he felt so hopelessly rooted to the ground that he could only stare at the entry in the dictionary and shake his head.

———

In the morning, Pretzel sits at the breakfast table poring over the business section of the *Times*. It is something he does every day, though the news of various mergers, takeovers, and new issues is as mysterious to him as the strange utterances that come from his mother's room late at night when she reads her Bible. He hopes that if he reads it often enough, something, some grain of wisdom, will become clear to him. So he plows ahead, though it feels futile —a language he was not meant to learn, like his mother, who in her desire to become even closer with God, practices speaking in tongues.

In the Business Opportunities section, he sees the ad. A Brooklyn tax practice, well-established, $200,000 average gross, then a phone number. Eps was right. Fishman is selling.

———

Like the bad weather that continues to spit gray drizzle down on the city, Ronnie seems to be everywhere. Pretzel finds him outside the liquor store. They take a walk over by the elevated shuttle stop and stand under the ancient, splintered wooden beams.

"What are you thinking?" he asks his brother.

Ronnie smiles at him. "I take it off you, that's all. We split it later."

"What if he don't believe it?"

"We'll do it right in front of his face, man. He watches you cross that street every night. I'm surprised you *ain't* been mugged."

Pretzel looks at the tops of his shoes, which he shines to perfection every morning, and wonders why he bothers. "All right," he says, quietly. "Tomorrow's Friday—payday. Lots of people picking up their returns."

"My man," says Ronnie, and puts out his hand, but Pretzel does not take it.

"I ain't doing this for you," he says.

———

Pretzel cuts out of school early and spends the afternoon in the park, walking and thinking. He could still call this off, no problem. He thinks over the conversations he's had with Fishman and sees that they fall into two categories: the ones that are purely business, like when he sends him out for supplies or talks about how much money came in, and the other times, when he talks about Pretzel's future.

Stopping to buy a hot dog, he watches bicyclists speed past in colorful clumps. A stray dog parks itself warily a few feet away and waits, watching him. Pretzel can see what will happen— Fishman won't say anything until the last minute, and then it'll be some fake sentiment, a twenty-dollar bill, a handshake, and the cheap smile he gives out fifty times a day, practiced over twenty-five years of dealing with ignorant clients. Feeling suddenly ill, Pretzel tosses the hot dog to the sidewalk, where the stray pounces and devours it in one fluid motion.

———

Friday, when Pretzel shows up at the office, Fishman is on the phone. "Good, you're here," he says, putting it down. "Do you know Johnny Bigelow?"

"Of course."

"I've been trying to call him, but he hasn't got a listed number."

"Got no phone."

Fishman throws up his hands. "That explains it. He overpaid by twenty dollars. I couldn't figure it, the receipts kept coming out twenty over, but then I narrowed it down to him. It was busy when he picked up, but still, you'd think these people would pay attention to their own money." He shakes his head.

Pretzel shrugs. "Drunk, probably. He always is when he comes down here."

Fishman sticks a twenty dollar bill in his hand. "Run this over to him, would you?"

Pretzel looks at the twenty. "Why?" he says. "He don't know."

Fishman looks at him directly for the first time since he has come in. "You know the answer to that, don't you?"

"No, I don't," he says. "You got the money in your hand. That's twenty more for you and nobody gets hurt."

"You are really something." Fishman sits at his desk and motions Pretzel to a chair in front of it. He sticks his hands deep into the pockets of his coat.

"Johnny Bigelow's been coming to this office for twenty years," says Fishman. "Since before you were born." He runs a hand through his thinning hair. He looks tired. "I provide a service here. It's not a pretty place, and I don't pretend it is. But I've never cheated anybody. If I make a mistake, I take responsibility."

"You don't care," says Pretzel.

"What do you mean? What's eating you?"

Pretzel faces him squarely. "You lied," he says. The look of concern on Fishman's face just makes Pretzel angrier. "You're selling."

Fishman raises his eyebrows. "I don't know for sure that I'm selling."

"I seen the ad."

He nods. "So? I thought I'd see what kind of offers I got. You want I should stay in this place forever? I'm getting old. Anyway, I haven't even had one call. Nobody wants this neighborhood."

"Seven years and you don't say nothing."

"Why should I? Is this your business? I like you, Pretzel, but come on. You want to be emptying my wastebaskets when you're fifty?" He puts two fingers to his forehead and squeezes momentarily. "I know you've got it tough, but that's all the more reason for you to try harder. You don't have to be like all the others."

They say nothing to each other for minutes. Finally, Pretzel stands and walks to the window. He can see Ronnie on the other side of the street, leaning against the side of a building, waiting. He walks back over to Fishman. "You want me to get the M.O.'s first?" he asks quietly.

Fishman looks at him for a moment, then shakes his head in frustration. "No, take Johnny back his twenty. Then the M.O.'s."

Expressionless, Pretzel nods, zips up his coat, and steps out the door.

———

As Fishman watches him go, he feels tired. He didn't tell Pretzel that, in fact, a man had offered him a decent price for the business that very morning, and he'd turned him down. He's not even sure why. He tries to summon the memory of this same street corner twenty-five years ago, but like the face of his first wife, it is something he has erased, and it is pointless to try. He does remember Pretzel though, skinny and wide-eyed, running errands for a quarter here and a dime there, and he wonders at how dependent he has become on the kid, as well as Pretzel on him. It was never meant to happen this way, but here he is playing father to a seventeen-year-old black kid, when his own children barely even keep in touch. It's a responsibility he doesn't need, and yet, like everything in his life, it has grown around him without his noticing, a twisting, painful vine that will, he fears, eventually choke the breath from him.

He leans against the thick, cold glass of the door and watches Pretzel cross the avenue, the streetlights illuminating the parka he bought him just last week. He could have bought a better one, had in fact planned to, but at the last moment he'd changed his mind. An expensive coat would have put things on a different level. All he really wanted was that the kid shouldn't freeze. It wasn't a gift, not really. Just essentials, that's all. But when he thinks of all the nice coats he could have bought him, an empty feeling scrapes his gut, and he feels tireder still.

When Pretzel has crossed the street, Ronnie comes over to him. "All right, man," he says, "Let's do it."

"I changed my mind," he tells him.

"You ain't changing nothing. Where is it?"

"You heard me. I got something to do."

Ronnie reaches to put a hand in his pocket, but Pretzel smacks it away.

"What's the matter?"

"Why'd you even come back here?"

"I live here." Ronnie grins broadly, exposing gums that have begun to recede.

"We got no business."

Ronnie nods, taking in the situation.

"Don't even try it," says Pretzel, turning away.

Suddenly he finds himself thrown up against the hard brick of a building, Ronnie's hand clamped against his throat. He gasps for breath, forgets the twenty dollars in his pocket, forgets Fishman and Johnny Bigelow and the money orders. His vision clouded by tears, he summons all his strength and kicks out straight and high, aiming right between Ronnie's legs.

Ronnie falls back astonished, and for a moment the two stand facing each other like wrestlers, each waiting for the other to move. Then Ronnie reaches into his boot and takes out a small kitchen knife.

A crowd has begun to gather, but they keep their distance. Across the street, Pretzel is aware of Fishman's face, framed in the window, watching. He should run, he thinks, run and keep running, but something makes him stand his ground. An empty MD 20/20 bottle lies next to the curb and he grabs it, busts the end off against the side of the building. The glass cuts the side of his hand, but he can't feel the pain, only the wetness of the blood on his hand.

Everywhere, people are watching him, waiting. In his state of mind, Pretzel forgets who he is, where he is, the fact that he does not even have the money. Eyes peer out from doorways, from the windows of the burnt-out buildings, and the street is filled with a sound of deeply drawn breath that may or may not be his own. The noise grows in intensity until it is a rumble, then a roar in his ears not unlike the crowd at a Knicks game, or the sound of the ocean. Ronnie comes at him, knife held low. The noise is deafening now, and shouting as loud as he can to drown it out, Pretzel swings high toward Ronnie's face, feels himself connect with the side of his head, feels for just a moment a wonderful satisfaction, as if he has solved an impossible math problem. Then a bright comet of pain in his side as the knife enters almost effortlessly, his head seems to come untethered from his body, and the sound suddenly goes away.

It takes a moment for Fishman to realize what is happening. He grabs the telephone and dials 911, shouting to the dispatcher to hurry. There have been muggings and fights out here before, even a shooting, and Fishman has always lowered the gates and waited until it is over. But this is Pretzel, and he can do nothing but watch in horror.

Fishman's view is blocked by the onlookers suddenly moving forward, and it is nearly a minute before he can see again. Pretzel is lying curled on the ground, his attacker gone. Almost as if they knew how long to wait, the police appear, stopping traffic and holding back the people. One of them comes over and knocks on the glass. Fishman unlocks.

"You saw what happened?" asks the cop.

"That's Pretzel," he says quietly. "He works for me." Big Larry has stepped into the office too. He walks around picking up staplers and putting them down.

"The other one?"

Fishman shakes his head. "He tried to mug him. Pretzel was returning twenty dollars to one of my clients. He was protecting the money." Shaken, he sits. "Twenty dollars," he says.

"A mugging?" says the cop skeptically. "Sure doesn't look like a mugging to me."

"What else?" asks Fishman.

"I don't know. Just seems like a hell of a lot of trouble to go to over twenty dollars. Your employees really that loyal?"

"Is he all right?"

The cop shakes his head. "Hard to say. EMS are checking him out now. He got knifed, hit his head too. Think your boy might have been on drugs?"

"Not Pretzel, no way."

"Well, we'll know soon enough. But don't fool yourself. These kids, they're all into something."

Big Larry drops a stapler and bends to pick it up. The cop points a finger at his chest.

"What about you, old man? You know anything about this?"

"Known 'em both since they was little."

"OK pal," says the cop, "You just won a free trip back to the precinct."

As he is led out the door, Big Larry looks back at Fishman and grins. "I'm a doctor," he tells him. "I'm a lawyer. I got thousands."

Across the street, behind the locked doors of his pharmacy, Fishman can see Eps in his white jacket, staring out on the scene.

———

Fishman sits for a long time in his car before he gets up the nerve to go to the door. Pretzel's mother answers, and from the expression on her face, he can see that she already knows.

"I'm sorry," he tells her. He fingers the envelope in his pocket, but does not take it out.

"You don't have to be, mister. I raised me one bad child. The Lord balance everything out in the end."

They stand in silence for a moment, and then Fishman asks, "May I come in?"

She nods and he steps inside, greeted by the calming scent of old, worn furniture, varnished wood floors, and a subtle hint of cleaning fluid. Everything immaculate and in its place, a cut glass candy dish full of M&M's on the table in front of the sofa. He sits.

"I only have a few minutes," she says. "My girlfriend is coming to give me a ride to the hospital. Would you like some coffee? Or a soda?"

"No thank you."

"My husband done his tax with you."

Fishman strains to remember, but cannot.

"Years ago," she says.

"We're none of us getting any younger."

"I want to thank you for the coat you bought my boy."

"It's nothing," says Fishman, embarrassed. "He's a good worker."

"He thinks a lot of you, too."

"Look, there's going to be hospital bills," says Fishman. "I want to help." He pulls out the stack of money from his pocket, the day's receipts that Pretzel never got to take to Eps.

"No," she says. "This ain't no charity case. What those two boys done they done by themselves. You just put that away."

Embarrassed, he begins to, but a thought strikes him, and he wonders why he didn't think of it before.

"Pretzel was working for me at the time of the fight — running an errand. He was injured on the job."

The doorbell rings. "Well," she says, "I suppose you know better than I do."

"Technically, I'm responsible." It is as if a light has been turned on somewhere in his head. He puts the money back in his pocket and takes out a business card. "You'll send me the medical bills. This is my home number. Please, let me know as soon as you find out how he is."

Fishman watches Pretzel's mother drive off with her friend, then gets in his own car. He sits for a minute, watching the drops of water gather slowly in front of him on the windshield, then under their collective weight, slide smoothly down the glass. His body feels tired and battered, as if he himself has been through some kind of fight this evening. Across the street he sees a man in torn and ill-fitting clothes with a tall, knit cap on, coming drunkenly toward him. Fishman locks his door and starts the engine, just as the man reaches the car. The man is trying the door as Fishman pulls out, and he very nearly knocks him over. A couple of yards further and a bottle smashes his back window, but Fishman does not stop. He drives as quickly as he can through the blocks and blocks of row houses, and on out to the expressway that will take him home to wait for the news.

# ERIN AND MALCOLM

E rin was in her stage clothes. Her black hair hung Chinese-style in a sharp curtain around her jaw, two inches shorter on the left. The haircut was new, but Malcolm hadn't said anything. The rest of her outfit was what she always wore: tight leather skirt, fishnet stockings, white tank top under a ripped jeans jacket, and enough bracelets to fill a shoe box. From one of her shoulders her pet ferret, Rizzo, eyed Malcolm with apparent contempt.

"I need the keys to the van," she said.

Malcolm got up and dug them out of the pocket of his other jeans. "Where are you playing tonight?"

"Brothers." Erin held out her hand, palm up.

"Are they paying anything yet?"

"Four." She twisted her nose as if this figure were of little consequence to her. "It's a hundred more than last time."

He tossed her the keys. "Just be careful. I noticed a scratch on the fender yesterday."

"It's not my fault. You know I'm a good driver."

"I'm just saying be careful is all."

She reached up and adjusted an earring, Rizzo slinking over to the other shoulder as she did so, then crouched down to Malcolm's level and looked out across the street at the hotel window he had been watching. A fat man in a T-shirt was standing with his hands on his hips. A woman passed in front of him and out of sight. "You're awful," she said. "What are they doing over there?"

"I don't know," he said. "What do you think they're doing?"

"Something strange. The guy is probably some kind of fetish. He wants her to lick his ankles, but she won't go for it."

"A person can't be a fetish," Malcolm told her. "You can have one, but you can't be one."

"All right," she said, standing. "You know what I meant."

———

When she was gone he went into the living room and took out his bass. It was the Fender Precision he'd bought just after marrying Erin, with money her father had given them for a wedding present. The finish was worn to the wood in many places, and it had acquired a lacquer of beer smell and cigarette smoke from fourteen months of nights in roadhouses and rock clubs. That was how long Malcolm had played in Erin's band while still keeping his contracting business going days. Then, six months ago, when he was renovating an apartment downtown, the circular saw he was using caught something in the wood and hopped into the V between his thumb and left forefinger, spattering blood and severing a tendon. He'd tied his shirt around it and walked, cursing, to the hospital.

The band hired a new bass player. Malcolm, his hand bandaged and unlikely ever really to be the same, had to watch their growing success from the other side of the stage. A friend of his in Vermont who was into some new variant of EST had told him everything that happens to you, you make happen — even little things like busy signals on the telephone, or headaches. Often he wondered what he had been thinking about just before he'd sawed into his hand. He tried to replay the event, but there was just gray space.

Hooking up a strap, he slipped the bass around his neck, plugged in to the ancient Ampeg that stood mute next to the stereo, turned it on and watched its tubes begin to glow. From his usual spot atop the television, curled around the antenna, Rizzo watched. Malcolm didn't care for the animal, or for the way Erin treated it. She'd bought the thing after the band started to do well, as a kind of lifestyle prop. To Malcolm, Rizzo represented everything about Erin that had changed lately — all the tacky theatrics. It was the same night she'd brought him home that she'd told Malcolm she needed to be by herself.

Something had gone wrong — he could see it in the way she looked at him over her morning bowl of cereal, and the way she didn't as she peeled herself out of her lycra pants and leopard shirts at night. Without ever actually discussing the problem, or even admitting to one, they'd sought remedies. Erin talked for a while about having a lesbian affair. Together, they'd made a serious attempt at vegetarianism. One Saturday night when the band was idle, they'd rented some porno movies, got drunk, and tried to watch them, but Erin only found them hilarious. Finally, by unspoken agreement, they'd given up. Erin brought Rizzo home and laid down the new rules. So, that's what they were doing now, living in the same place, being by themselves.

There was no single moment you could trace it to, not even the accident with the saw. Rather, it had been a steady process. It was how things happened, Malcolm thought, as he thumped a string and listened to the sound grow in the speaker. Not suddenly, the way you expected them to, but in increments and shadings you could never quite put your finger on.

Malcolm had about ten grand invested in the van and the PA system, which the band continued to use. In return, Erin paid the rent. Malcolm watched a lot of television these days, sitting coldly in front of the screen with a Big Buckeroo dart gun in his hand, firing point-blank at sitcoms with their smiling husbands and career-girl wives. A teacher of his had once explained the theory of an expanding universe as a raisin cake baking in an oven, with the raisins remaining in one place while everything around them moved outward at equal speed. This was just how he felt—immobile, like a raisin.

He popped a cassette into the tape deck and the room filled with crowd noises, the clatter of beers being set down, a jumble of voices. Then the sound of a guitar string being tuned to pitch, and suddenly the whole band slamming into gear. Forcing his fingers against the strings, Malcolm banged along. He liked playing to these old tapes, but didn't do it when Erin was around. If he closed his eyes, it was almost like being there all over again. He had the tapes memorized, even the little screwups, the missed beats, the wrong notes. They didn't bother him anymore. He had heard them so often that when they came up, they seemed like old friends.

Usually, Rizzo left the room when Malcolm started to play, curling himself up on Erin's bed. But this evening he arced his back and hopped off the television onto the floor, where he stood looking at him.

"Rodent," said Malcolm. He cranked the volume on the bass, hoping to drive him out of the room. Rizzo traced a figure eight on the floor, then hopped back up onto the television by way of the empty box from the CD player Erin had just bought. Malcolm went over to the amp and turned it up to six. He could hear the thing humming. He shut all the doors leading out of the room and turned off the tape deck, then faced Rizzo and smiled. "How y'all feeling tonight?" he said. "Anybody want to rock and roll?"

He hit an open A that shook the floorboards, and the effect on the ferret was visible. His hair seemed to puff out an inch on all sides, and he drew himself back into a question mark.

Malcolm sang as loud as he could, "I said, Hey, bartender . . ."

Rizzo was now flat against the wall, looking nervously around for an escape. Malcolm began a boogie bass line that was so loud a phantom rhythm section of pots and pans began shivering in accompaniment from the kitchen. The animal hopped back and forth, almost as if to the music, but in obvious distress. It wasn't enough volume for Malcolm. Backing up to the amplifier, he spun the knob to ten.

"I want you all to put your hands together for this one," he said. He went over to Rizzo and held the instrument practically in front of his nose.

It was only one note, and it only lasted a second, but the sound was like a bomb going off. The apartment lights flickered for a moment. Then the speaker expired with a tired raspberry, and a panicked Rizzo, fearing for his life, first sunk his teeth into the back of Malcolm's hand, then hopped up onto the stereo system and from there, out the open window.

"Damn," said Malcolm, grabbing at his re-injured hand. He went to the window and looked down to see where Rizzo had landed, but the animal was nowhere in sight. Fifteen feet below was another roof that jutted out from the side of the building, covered with garbage: old boxes, empty cans and bottles, a rotting mattress. From there it was another forty feet or so to the ground, an alley that ran behind the building.

He held his hand under his armpit and wondered what to do. It hadn't occurred to him that there might be consequences to his actions. He wondered if he could tell Erin Rizzo had jumped for no reason at all. She would never believe it. But it wasn't necessarily his fault. And besides, the little bastard had bitten him. He was probably going to contract some horrible ferret disease. He imagined his arm swelling up like a long black balloon, the kind magicians twist into animals at parties.

He went into the kitchen, ran hot water over his hand, and taped some gauze over it. Then he hunted through the cabinets, finally settling on a can of tuna, which he opened and brought back to the window. "Here, little buddy," he said. "I've got something for you."

He waved the can in the air to spread its aroma, then called out again, directing his words to the deteriorating clumps of trash below. "Come on, I've got some nice tuna here." It felt idiotic to be talking this way. He thought of Erin and how she held long conversations with Rizzo as he sat on her shoulder, feeding him morsels of cheese and rubbing his small, weasel nose with her finger.

"I'm sorry," he tried again. "I was just fooling around." He looked above him and saw a man standing at a window, watching. Malcolm smiled, then pulled his head back in. He stuck the can of tuna in the refrigerator, pulled on his boots, and went out.

Though a tiny animal, Rizzo had left an easy trail to follow. At the Korean grocery across the street a woman sat surprised on the sidewalk, cantaloupes positioned around her like pool balls after a break shot. The grocer held a broom in his hand, ready to strike at the first sign of the demon that had invaded his store. His wife waved her hands and tried to calm the other customers in broken English. At the far end of the block, a man walking his Afghan was nearly pulled out into the street as the dog began barking and straining at his leash. Malcolm ran toward them.

The dog was barking up an alleyway and Malcolm turned in, trying to move calmly so as not to scare Rizzo. There were kitchen entrances on either side, one for a Chinese take-out place, the other a Mexican restaurant where he had once eaten with Erin and gotten sick from some bad sour cream. He paused between the two, wondering what his next step ought to be. He wasn't even sure Rizzo would come to him. From inside the Mexican restaurant there was the sound of a large pan hitting the floor, followed by shouting in Spanish. Malcolm pushed open the screen door.

Three cooks were yelling instructions at each other. One of them held an iron skillet over his head. From high on a pantry shelf, Rizzo hung his pointed face down, his red eyes gleaming with what Malcolm was sure was pleasure.

"Rizzo," said Malcolm in the sternest tone he could muster. "Come." For nearly a year when he was a kid he had tried to teach a small mongrel dog to respond with this same command, before his parents had finally given the pet away. "Come here," he said, his voice even lower.

The cook with the frying pan had been sneaking over from the side and was now in position to try a smack at the ferret, but Rizzo saw him coming and dove in the opposite direction, toward the stove. Beyond that was the entrance to the dining room. But he miscalculated just a bit, and landed on a saucepan lid that was balanced precariously above the stove. It tipped and fell taking Rizzo with it, depositing him neatly into a vat of deep-frying oil.

Malcolm had to give the chef ten bucks before he would let him fish Rizzo out and take him home. They gave him a carryout sack with *Andale Andale*, the name of the restaurant, printed on it, and he walked back to the apartment feeling sick. Once inside, he put Rizzo in his customary place atop the television, opened himself a diet root beer, sat down and stared at the blank screen.

———

He was asleep when she came in, his head dangling off the side of the chair. The sounds she made woke him. Disoriented, he was sure the apartment was being burglarized and jumped to his feet. Then he remembered.

"Babe," said Erin when she saw he was awake, "Have you seen Rizzo?"

"He's on the television," said Malcolm, but even as he said it he saw that the bag was gone.

Erin noticed his expression. "I stuck your leftovers in the fridge," she said. "You can't leave food out like that. It will spoil." She walked around the room, looking behind the furniture for signs of her pet. "I can't believe you went back to that place after you got so sick the last time."

Malcolm watched her move, trying to remember how it used to feel to look at her. When they'd first met she had seemed so mysterious and intriguing, like a carefully wrapped present delivered to him by mistake.

She noticed his bandage. "What did you do to your hand?"

"Erin," he said. "You'd better sit down."

She took it fairly well, considering. She listened calmly, knitting her brows in concentration, occasionally pulling at the one earring she had forgotten to take off. Then she went into the bathroom and threw up. Malcolm got the bag out of the refrigerator and put it on the table. When she came out he was standing in front of it, his hands in his pockets.

"I just don't understand," she said.

"Maybe he saw something out there."

"Out *that* window?"

"Well, maybe he was trying to follow you." Malcolm's bass was still out, and he went to put it away. "What do you want to do with him?"

"I don't know," she said. "I can't think." She touched the bag tentatively with one finger, then pulled back. "Did you have to bring him back like *this?*"

"Would you rather I'd just left him?"

"Yes," she said. "This is so gruesome."

"Well, I'm sorry," said Malcolm. "I'll take him out to the dumpster. I just thought you might want to do something. Bury him or something." He picked up the bag.

"Wait a minute," said Erin. "We can't just throw him out like a piece of garbage. You're right. We should bury him."

Malcolm put the bag back down. "OK," he said. "I've done my part. I'm going to bed."

She nodded. He went behind his partition, took off his shirt, and lay down.

A half-hour passed during which Malcolm looked up in the darkness at the ceiling and tried unsuccessfully to will himself to sleep. He'd done all he could, more even, he thought. But still he couldn't rid his mind of the image of the white take-out sack on the table in the other room.

He heard footsteps. Erin was standing in his doorway. "Malcolm?" she said. "I need help."

"What do you mean?"

"I don't know where to take him."

"What am I supposed to do?"

"Come on. Can't you see I'm upset?"

She was actually asking him for something besides the truck keys, for the first time in a long time. Malcolm realized that, in an odd way, he was enjoying this — enjoying the power.

"He was your pet," he said.

"Malcolm, please." She seemed on the verge of tears. He thought back to the first job the band had played, and how she'd suddenly come down with nervous diarrhea an hour before the show. He'd had to make a last minute run to the drugstore to get her medicine.

The carpenter in him began turning the situation over, considering the angles. There was always a solution if you looked hard enough.

"We could call the ASPCA," he said. "Or a vet. They have to dispose of dead pets all the time."

"I want to bury him," she said.

"All right. So what we need to do is find a place. Some grass or something. How about Central Park?"

"I want it to be close."

He considered. "That's tough. It's not like we have a backyard." He glanced out the window at the Towne House Hotel, the outside of which he'd spent so many hours staring at that each dingy brick was ingrained in his mind. "I know," he said.

———

The night clerk at the hotel was staring lizardlike into a portable black-and-white television, and barely looked at them as they signed the register. Malcolm's idea was that by taking a room they would have access to the hotel's rooftop garden. He knew they had one, because a yellowing tin sign by the entrance proclaimed the fact. They would bury Rizzo, then sneak out so they wouldn't have to pay. He signed the register "Les Paul," and Erin, playing out the joke, signed underneath it "Mary Ford." He liked her for that, for knowing him so well. He also felt the guilt again, as if it were something heavy he'd swallowed. Malcolm carried a small overnight case containing Rizzo's remains, along with a spatula and a large serving spoon to use as digging implements since they had no shovel.

"Payment in advance," said the desk clerk in a bored voice.

Malcolm made a show of patting his pockets. "Damn," he said. "I must have left my wallet in the car."

The clerk just looked at him. He had the pasty complexion of someone who spent his days asleep and his nights in front of a TV.

"The car's in the garage for the night. I won't be able to get to it until morning. You can trust us." Malcolm smiled as broadly as he could, but was conscious that in his jeans and T-shirt, an earring in his ear, he looked very un-touristlike.

"Welcome to New York," said the clerk. "Nobody trusts nobody here. You give me some money, you get a room." He yawned and turned back to the television.

"Wait a minute," said Erin. "I think I may have some cash." She dug into her pants pocket and pulled out a wad of bills — her evening's pay. She counted out the amount for the room, nearly all she had.

"The grocery money, darling," she said, taking his arm. "I forgot to give it to the maid."

The clerk eyed her without amusement, then took a key off a hook. "Three-seventeen," he said. "Need help with your bags?"

"No, I got 'em," said Malcolm.

"Elevator to the third floor, turn right. Checkout is eleven-thirty." He turned back to his television.

"I'm broke," said Malcolm when they were on the elevator. "I can't split this with you."

"It's OK," she said. " This is cheap, relatively. When my aunt died, my Uncle Bob spent over three grand on the funeral, and that wasn't even New York."

They bypassed the third floor and went straight to the top of the building, got off and climbed a short flight of stairs to a metal door that led onto the roof.

"It figures," said Malcolm when he pushed it open.

The rooftop garden was not really a garden at all, but a paved deck with a few lounge chairs scattered about and some potted plants. There wasn't a square foot of grass. The moon hung like a dinner plate over the dark contours of the city, bathing the concrete in a thin gray light. He walked over to the railing and looked down. The view was dizzying — a constellation of intersecting planes going down a straight drop of two hundred feet.

"Romantic, isn't it?" said Erin, coming over to join him and pointing up. "You could almost reach up and touch it. Don't feel bad. It was a good idea."

He tightened his grip on the railing. He wanted to confess, but the words would not come.

"There," said Erin. She was pointing at a potted tree, a palm of some sort.

"What?" said Malcolm.

"We'll bury him there. Right in with that tree. There's plenty of room." Her expression was practical, her voice calm and measured. She might have been discussing the weather.

She used the spatula and Malcolm helped with the spoon. They worked around the tree's roots, and managed in a few minutes to clear a space of roughly Rizzo's proportions. Malcolm watched her slender fingers as they worked the dirt. A pale line still marked the place where she'd stopped wearing her ring. When they were done it was with great hesitation that he finally brought out the paper bag.

"Maybe we should say something," Erin said, looking dubiously, first at it, then at the hole they had dug. "Malcolm?"

"You say something."

She put a hand to her forehead and closed her eyes. "OK," she said. "Dear Lord, we are gathered here to say good-bye to one of your creatures, a ferret, Rizzo by name."

Malcolm watched a tear form in the corner of her eye.

"I feel stupid," she said.

"Don't," he told her.

She took a breath and continued. "He was a good pet. I don't know why he would have run off like he did, but he did." She looked down at her feet, as if some additional words might be written there. "I hope you can find space for Rizzo in heaven Lord. He's not very big." Taking the spatula, she motioned for Malcolm to empty the ferret, who was quite stiff by now, into the pot. Then she turned earth over him until he was completely covered.

They walked in silence back to the elevator, which whirred and clanked its way up to them, then opened its doors with a gasp like a swimmer coming up for air.

Erin pressed the button for the third floor. The doors opened onto a dingy hallway that smelled of cleaning fluid and old closets.

"You're going to stay?" Malcolm asked. His voice sounded loud in the empty hall.

"Seems like a waste of money not to, and I don't know, I don't like the idea of going back to an empty apartment."

He stared at her.

"Rizzo's on his way to heaven, right now."

Malcolm, one hand in his pocket, ran his thumbnail up and down along the edge of a quarter.

"You can stay too," she offered. "I don't mind."

As they entered the room together, Malcolm suddenly found himself wondering about the desk clerk downstairs, and what he really thought. That Erin was a hooker Malcolm had purchased for the evening? That they were criminals of some sort, laying low? Or maybe adulterers in need of a place to have their affair. In the dim light, he watched Erin's tired movements as she walked about the room, touching things with her outstretched finger — the dresser, a floor lamp, the edge of the bed — as if this gesture were enough to make the place home. A desk clerk at a place like this would see a lot, he thought. After a while, you'd stop trying to guess and just accept things at face value. As far as that guy downstairs was concerned, Malcolm and Erin were exactly what they represented themselves to be — a married couple looking for a room for the night. The details were no one's business. It was easier that way.

# DOWN AT THE STUDIO

The answering machine is on the blink, but I've got the door to the booth open, so I hear the phone. I figure it is probably Dave, stuck someplace, needing a ride home. Since he dried out, he has occasional moments when he seizes up, like an engine with no oil. The last time was two weeks ago, when he got off the train at Fourth Avenue, then couldn't get himself to leave the station.

"Nick and Dave's," I say, hating the name, which still sounds to me like a pizza parlor. "What?"

"Nick? It's Betsy."

She's been gone six years, but her tone of voice is like she calls all the time.

"Is Dave around?"

"Nope," I say. "Where are you?"

"Right here, in Brooklyn. I moved back. I got my own place, and I'm taking acting classes."

I can see it. She's tall, and if she's kept her looks, she'll probably have a shot at commercials or something.

"He's probably at the Sham," she says. "I'll go look for him. Buy him a drink."

"He drinks sodas these days. Coca-Cola, mostly."

"Dave?"

"Just goes down for company, anymore." The Shamrock is the last real bar in the neighborhood—the only one left that hasn't installed ferns and a CD player. Older guys go there, and the softball teams. Sometimes a young couple will stroll in and have a beer, but it's only comfortable if you know everyone, and have known them all your life. Dave has his own booth, and a special set of darts they keep for him in the register. If they're shorthanded, he might even tend a little bar.

There is a long silence at the other end, and in it I imagine a whole scenario for Betsy—a place on the beach, shiny cars, palm trees.

"How's business?" she asks, finally.

"OK," I say. "Listen, Betsy, I'm in the middle of something, and it's kind of late."

After I hang up, I take a bite from a cold slice of Sicilian I picked up on my midnight break, wash it down with room temperature coffee, and go back into the booth. It's peaceful inside, all the equipment on and silent, the tiny lights looking out on me from everywhere like red, green, and blue eyes. The big eight-track, the half-inch Otari for mixdown, the effects rack standing cool and ready next to the centerpiece, my mixing board, sixteen channels with knobs that go on forever. A momentary shudder in the power source has left the digital readout on the clock flashing in distress, but it doesn't matter. In the studio, time takes on different proportions, expanding and contracting in relation to your state of mind. Lately I've begun to feel like one of those sleep-deprivation experiments. Sunlight, when I find myself in it, always seems a little strange, like it shouldn't really be happening.

On one of our control sheets I print Dave a note, then take it to the office where he'll be sure to find it. We're on the top floor. There's a kindergarten in the basement, church offices on the first, and Dave lives on the second. Our studio is rent-free — barter for his caretaking the building. We insulated nearly two feet thick so there wouldn't be a noise problem.

At the front gate, I see him coming down the street, hands sunk deep in his pockets, his pace slow and steady. He looks like he ought to have a can to kick, eyes focused down on the sidewalk. I slip out quickly and go the opposite direction.

———

Lunchtime the next day, Dave's eating a meatball sandwich, and I notice tiny flecks of red on the appointment book, which is to one side of him, so I move it.

"What did Betsy want?" I ask.

"She needs a loft for her apartment," he says through a mouthful. Dave is a good carpenter. He built the studio, really, though I was there to hammer nails and haul lumber. Since we got it finished he's been obviously bored. Taking another bite from the sandwich, he uses one finger to reposition a meatball that is trying to escape from the far end.

"She going to pay you?"

He nods. "I'm going over there to take a look in a few minutes."

He has already been making sketches. In front of him there is a sheet of paper with some rough outlines penciled on it.

"You've got Neon Maniacs at four," I say, flipping through the book.

"Just a rehearsal. I told them I'd roll some tape. Cover for me, would you?"

"All right, but I've got Motion Sickness again after dinner, so they can't run overtime."

Our deal is that we each bring in our own business, engineer our own sessions. But I'm always having to do final mixes for him, or run off copies he forgot to make, and it worries me. His whole life, he's never stuck with anything long. He had three or four bands himself that all fell apart. Simple lack of interest.

He smiles and gets up. "Thanks, bro." He slips on his leather jacket and heads out.

I collect his garbage off the desk, crunch the foil up into a ball, slipping it inside the paper bag, and drop it in the trash.

———

For about a month when he was sixteen and I was twelve, Dave changed his name to Ian. It was Betsy who suggested it. He was in an English rock phase, and played in a Yes copy band. I was in training for a position with the New York Jets; I high-stepped through the park afternoons, dodged imaginary tacklers, swung by my arms from playground equipment with the idea that stretching might somehow make me taller. I could do seventy push-ups. I didn't think much of my brother, or the miniature domino he wore dangling from one ear.

"Ian?" I said when he told me. "You've got to be kidding."

"Don't mess with me, Nick-wit," he said. "There's nothing wrong with having a stage name."

"Of course not," said Betsy. They were sitting on the stoop together outside the deli her father owned before he died. She had new glasses on — round ones that made her look considerably older. I was filled with contempt. Two seriously misled people — it seemed to me they deserved each other.

"Sure," I said. "Ian. Right."

Betsy stuck her tongue out at me, managing somehow to look good doing it. Shaking my head, I turned around and fell right over my bicycle. There was no graceful way out — I was tangled in the thing, and my knee stung where I'd skinned it.

"You're fooling yourselves," I said loudly at the sidewalk, ignoring their laughter. It seemed the worst thing I could come up with. But I couldn't hurt them, and I knew it. They traveled in their own little world, and though I could peer in from outside, I could never really enter.

———

Dave's session turns out to be five neighborhood kids who've just smoked a bunch of dope — their eyes are closed up tight as newborn pups, and they reek like a Rastafarian picnic. They don't even bother to tune, just plug in and start banging away. The singer is making it up as he goes along. He runs his fingers violently through his hair when he's not shouting at the mike, a gesture that isn't for anyone's benefit I can see, except maybe mine, since the rest of the band are staring in different directions. The drummer watches a blank spot on the wall, the guitarist seems to be counting the eyelets on his boots. The endings of their songs take longer than the songs themselves.

I make the mistake of offering to let them hear the tape, and have to watch as they listen to every nuance. Finally, against my better judgment, I leave them alone in the booth. It's just a simple stereo recording — two ambient mikes hung in the room, taped onto a sixty-minute cassette — but they listen to it like it was a sermon.

One of these days some local group will walk in here and be really hot. They'll need good production, and I'll be available. It happens. There are springboards into the business.

For rehearsals we charge twenty, and Neon Maniacs pay me with a ten, eight ones, and a handful of change I don't bother to count. I let them go, wait about two minutes so I won't run into them, then lock up and hurry to the corner for a sandwich and soda. I have about ten minutes before the next session.

Poison Witness are commercial hard rockers, very serious about what they do, aiming for the jugular vein of the spandex-and-leather market. It was Dave who started calling them Motion Sickness, but the fact is that they're good. Their guitar player, Marty Bucknell, is a tall, handsome kid from the neighborhood who's cut from just the right mold, and knows it. Teased hair, sculpted face with high cheekbones, prominent jaw, and a mouth that would look almost feminine, if it wasn't twisted, just slightly, by a scar on one side. I wonder sometimes if he gave it to himself. He knows lots of tricks — two-handed tapping style, super-fast pick technique. His drummer and bass player are a little sloppy, and the drummer shouldn't be singing, but Marty has real potential.

They arrive while I'm still eating my sandwich, and Betsy is with them.

"Hey, Nick," she says. She's wearing a V-necked T-shirt and lycra stretch pants that hug her long legs like twin blue snakeskins. Spike heels. Her face has aged a bit, but when she smiles it's as though something lifts and she's the same weird, skinny girl who sold me my first kiss, in the back of her dad's store, surrounded by cases of canned goods. It lasted about ten seconds, cost me two bucks, and tasted of mint from the gum she constantly chewed.

She perches on the desk and takes a cigarette from her bag, her breasts clearly visible as she digs for a lighter.

"You guys know each other?" asks Marty.

"We grew up together," says Betsy, lighting up. "I can smoke, can't I?"

I get the ashtray out of the drawer.

"Nick's brother is the one who's going to build me the loft."

Marty nods, but he doesn't file it anywhere. Marty is only interested in things that apply directly to Marty.

She excuses herself to go to the bathroom, and Marty grabs a handful of my potato chips.

"Met her at the Sham last night," he says, by way of explanation. "Nice kid."

During the session she sits quietly behind me in the booth, sipping at a can of soda. I can see her reflection in the glass, legs folded, the image transparent, superimposed over Marty and the band. Finally, she leans forward and pokes the back of my neck.

"You're not saying anything. You might at least make small talk. Hi, Betsy. How are you Betsy? What's new with you?"

I bring down the monitors and turn. "Did you see Dave?"

She nods. "He was by this afternoon to take measurements. My place is really tiny, but high ceilings. It's going to be nice. He's designed a desk and bookshelves right into it, and a little stepladder, and I've got a futon for on top." Her eyes focus on Marty.

"Good-looking guy," I say.

She shrugs. "Kinda dumb, if you ask me."

The drummer has turned the beat around accidently — he's playing the one where the two should be. I have to stop the tape and call in the bad news. Behind me, Betsy crosses her legs the other way.

"Nick, Nick, Nick," she says. "Always the perfectionist."

Reaching a hand out, she musses my hair, then runs her fingernails lightly over the nape of my neck.

———

At the Sham, I find Dave about to win at darts. I watch him, the intense concentration on his face, the tension in the muscles of his arm, all of them poised for this, his last shot. When he actually throws it, it's just a flick of the wrist, as if he didn't really care where it landed. It's perfect though, double threes.

"How are things in the land of loud?" he asks, walking me to the bar.

I get a beer, and another Coke for him. "I want to talk to you," I say.

"About what?"

"The studio. You're not doing enough."

"That's not true. I did some sessions last week." He's taller than I am, a fact I'm rarely conscious of, except when we're in the Sham. I hold up fingers.

"Two. I don't mean to push you or anything, but we're in business. Now I see you jumping to build this thing for Betsy."

I never talk to him about Betsy—it's a major sore spot. He's gone out with other women since, but he never got over her. Betsy broke him. When she left, she didn't even say she was going, just got on a plane. She left instructions with her mother not to give out her new address. Something had come up, an "opportunity"— that was all he was able to find out. When he finally did get an address out of one of her friends, it didn't help. His letters came back unanswered.

He smiles and sips from his drink. "I'm going up to her place in about a half-hour."

All I can think of is I hope he doesn't bump into Marty on his way out. "Dave, don't be stupid. The woman is basic, unadulterated trouble, and if you can't see that then someone ought to give you a stick and some dark glasses."

"What is this, a warning?"

"No, advice. You're not strong enough for her."

"Me plenty strong," he says. "Me eat red meat, much potato. Me lift-em weights." On the television over the bar, women in bikinis are running over burning coals. "California hot-foot," says Dave, pointing.

I leave my half-finished beer in front of him and walk home.

———

The next few days I spend almost entirely in the studio, and all I see of Dave is his occasional face at the door telling me to hang in there. I have to admit though, he looks happy. I've got my own project going, a commercial for a dog food company I'm doing on spec for a guy I know that works at an agency. He says they always need stuff like this, I could make good money. My skin feels pasty, and from all the time in the dark, I am starting to squint like a mole.

When Betsy comes by three nights later, I have just cut my finger doing a splice. She carries a six-pack in a paper bag. "Nick-wit," she says. "What a mess."

In the bathroom we run it under cold water, turning the basin rust-red. Taking a Band-Aid from the medicine cabinet, she wraps it around my finger.

"You work too much," she tells me. In the small room we are practically touching. She leans forward and we kiss, carefully at first, then harder. I try to say something, like maybe how this isn't such a great idea, but she just puts a finger to her lips. "Don't talk," she says. "Not a word."

———

Later, I walk Betsy home, and along the way, she tells me about her voice teacher who thinks she definitely has a Broadway sound, which may or may not be a good thing, what with the decline of the American musical. She invites me in, and there it is, in the middle of the room, nearly completed. The loft is all oak, except for the desk underneath, which is some darker wood, mahogany, I think. Each piece has been lovingly sanded, and a can of stain sits on some newspaper, waiting to be applied. Still, there is something that isn't quite right. Empty cabinets for drawers hang under the desktop, and there is an adjoining counter area.

The apartment is only two rooms, and she's got no other furniture. Her clothes are in open suitcases. There is a package of eight-by-tens of her, ready for taking to auditions. Copies of *Backstage* and the *Voice* lie scattered on the floor.

"It doesn't look like you plan to stay," I say.

"I'm just settling in slowly. The loft is the centerpiece of the whole place. I can't do anything else until it's finished."

I touch one of the supports, realizing that this is without a doubt the best thing I've seen Dave do. But it hits me, too, what the problem is. The structure is simply too big for the space — it crowds the room. I've been thinking about whether or not to kiss her good-night, but now it seems out of the question.

"I'm meeting him in about an hour down at the Sham."

I don't say anything. Outside, there is some kind of accident going on. Flashing lights sweep across the walls.

"Dave and I have an understanding," she says. "It's never love after you say it isn't." She walks over to the window and looks down on the street.

———

I'm not sure how he found out, but when I come in the next evening, Dave's in the booth with the door locked. He's got a big bottle of Bushmills with him, but unopened. I tap on the glass and he looks up.

"How about letting me in?" I say.

He lights a cigarette, a move calculated to irritate me, since I don't allow smoking in the booth.

"Let's talk."

He cups a hand to one ear.

"Talk!" I shout.

Holding one finger up for me to be patient, he finds the switch on the board that allows me to hear him. His voice comes over the PA speakers, flat and cool.

"I'm working." Letting the switch up, he leans back and kicks up his feet.

Looking at Dave through the glass, I recognize the same red-eyed glare our dad gets when he's drinking — like coals simmering inside his head. The old man nearly choked laughing when he heard we were going into business together. My mother thought it was a great idea, but he just pronounced us fools.

"I give it six months," he said. "You go into business, you're agreeing to distrust another person. That's what business is, mutual distrust. You think the two of you are ready for that? You don't have the balls."

This goes on for a while, the two of us ignoring each other. I start pulling some duct tape off the carpet and rolling it up in my hand. At one point Dave throws the switch and the speakers come alive, hissing, waiting, and I think he's going to say something. But he just shuts them off again.

After a while he picks up a reel of tape and puts it on the machine, but doesn't switch on the mains, so I can't hear. He's wearing headphones, and I can see him chuckling to himself. I'm wondering whether it isn't time to give up and let the sonofabitch stew on his own. Going to the window, I tap on the glass. He doesn't hear me, only puts his feet up on the board, laughing harder. I knock again.

Still grinning, he rewinds and puts the speakers on. This is what comes out:

> Full of meat, mmmm, Mighty Pup!
> An eatin' treat, they'll eat . . . it . . . up!

The voice is mine — there are four renditions of the jingle, each a little different from the last, the accompaniment a simple drum machine beat overlaid with synth chords, bass, and some happy dog woofs I lifted off a sound effects album. There's no reason for it, but still, I feel violated, as if my jingle were a diary entry, or a confessional poem.

In the booth, Dave has got both hands on the machine now, rocking the reels back and forth so that one syllable is repeated backward and forward, over and over, a kind of scratch effect, probably damaging the motor. Without even thinking what I'm doing, I really hit the window. I hit it so hard even I am surprised, and the thick, stiff glass gives way, disintegrating around my fist.

Dave gets a roll of paper toweling to blot the blood that seeps from the side of my hand, and insists on walking me to the hospital, though I tell him I'm sure it's not serious.

"Mighty Pup?" he asks.

"I'm sorry," I say, meaning Betsy. "I don't know what happened."

"What happened is clear," he says. "The question is, why."

We walk together over to Mercy Hospital. At the ER he waits the whole time, even though public places, and hospitals in particular, make him nervous. A month in detox will do that.

All they do is bandage the hand. When the nurse asks me the cause of injury, for their records, I tell her self-inflicted.

"Come on," she says, smiling. "Would someone do a thing like this to themselves?"

———

Dave spends most of the weekend in Times Square, seeing movies, eating hamburgers, and playing video games. It's a way of not drinking for him. Monday morning he comes in and begins fixing the window in the booth. He starts talking about building a platform too, for the drums, but then he drifts into a whole thing about the cost of lumber, and I can see it's just talk.

Neither of us mention her. The fact that she doesn't seem to be around makes it easier, but it's still this big, unspoken thing between us. I start to think about maybe buying Dave's half of the business and moving the whole operation to my basement.

A couple days later, I find out from Marty that Betsy has gone back to the West Coast. Apparently, she got a call about a possible small part in a film.

"Very strange chick," he says. "You know what she did? She hung my guitar off the fire escape. Really. So I go out to get it, wearing only my underwear, and she shuts the window behind me. I guess she thought it was funny or something. Twenty minutes she kept me out there."

I imagine Marty pleading with Betsy to get back in and have to blow my nose.

"Strange sense of humor, that girl," he says.

A card comes in the mail, addressed to me and Dave. "Greetings from L.A.," it says. The picture is modern, but staged to look early sixties, three women in identical polka-dot bikinis, seated on a beach blanket, wearing straw hats and rhinestone sunglasses. The other side says only, "Dear guys, I miss you both. Take care, Betsy." I leave the card out on the desk for Dave, but he doesn't touch it, so it sits for days, gradually getting covered up by other papers, until all that shows is a strip of impossibly blue sky poking out between the phone and ConEd bills.

Not long after, I'm walking along the sidewalk outside of her building, and I see a pile of wood out by the curb. A small, dark man is bringing more down, and I stop him to ask about it.

"The old tenant," he says. "She build a bed into wall. No good for rent apartment again." He looks at me, calculating my interest, then shrugs. "You want," he says. "Take."

And I do. I gather as much of the heavy wood as I can carry, cradle it against my chest and walk back toward the studio. The oak is smooth and cool, though there are gouges and bent nails in places where it was ripped apart. I have to make a few trips to get it all. The work is tiring, but it's a nice day, and I'm glad to be outside in the air for a change. Picking up the two-by-fours one at a time, I position my hands carefully so they won't get cut. When I get it all back to the studio what I have is a great, disorderly pile. I sit down on the carpet, cross my legs, and watch it for a while, trying to figure out what it looks like, or what, with a little imagination, it might become.

# DADDY D. AND SHORT TIME

Christine came back to the truck to tell Ray a dwarf had moved into number two-nineteen. Well, maybe not a dwarf exactly—but a very little man with a fat belly, normal-sized head, and nearly useless legs. He had a big black guy helping him out.

"Uh-huh," said Ray, taking a bite from a peanut butter sandwich.

"Don't you think that's strange?" She opened one of the packs of cigarettes she'd bought from the Arab grocery at the end of the block.

He shrugged. "Lahla black 'roun' here," he said through the peanut butter.

[ 129

"Not the black guy, the dwarf." She watched as he chased the peanut butter with a swallow of milk from the carton, then flipped a page of the computer magazine he was looking at, even though he didn't know the first thing about computers. He was deliberately being a pain, and Dolly had turned into a real mess. There were crumpled candy wrappers and used paper plates everywhere. All four ashtrays were filled to overflowing with the stubs of Lucky Strikes. They'd been living in the truck for nearly three weeks now, the past two days parked in the middle of a block in what Ray had dubbed "Nigeria," a section of Brooklyn darker than anyplace Christine had ever been. The dwarf was about the first white person she'd seen since they'd come.

Two days earlier, a man had sold Ray ten mint-condition Gibson ES-155 electric guitars at two hundred and fifty dollars apiece —all the money they'd made selling Christmas trees. He'd had pomaded hair, two gold teeth in front, and a big smile. His name was K.C. and his voice was like an ad for some Caribbean airline— it sounded good enough to eat. Ray ran into him outside Manny's Music, where they were both admiring the window display, then made the deal without even discussing it with her, mysteriously driving them crosstown to an area of rotting piers and abandoned cars where K.C. had his station wagon parked. They took delivery of the instruments and K.C. gave them a business card, saying they should look him up next time they were in town.

It was Christine who'd insisted on taking one of the instruments down to We Buy Guitars, where they'd discovered, too late, that what they'd bought were Jap copies from the late sixties with Gibson decals pasted onto the headstocks. Value, a hundred apiece, tops.

Ray showed no emotion over the news, only nodded his head, internalizing the blow. But now he had them camped in front of the address on K.C.'s card, waiting. Christine had tried to point out that since K.C. lied about the guitars, it was more than likely the address was a fake too, but Ray wasn't listening.

Ray never listened. He might seem to be, but in the end he did things his own way, regardless. They'd met nearly a year ago when he was still running a college bookstore in Orono, Maine, and she was working at a little import place called Stallion Motors. She needed a new Chilton's to replace one of hers that had fallen completely apart.

"You fix cars?" he'd asked, his eyes straying to her hands which were smudged with grease.

"Cars, motorcycles, outboard motors, lawn mowers, you name it," she said. "Bicycles too, if I have the time." She was wearing her cowboy boots with the silver toe caps that day.

"Maybe you could come work on my truck." He never took his eyes off hers. His shoulder-length hair was tied back in a ponytail, and he wore a small turquoise earring in one ear. She thought he was cute, but it annoyed her to be flirted with, and she wondered if he even had a truck.

"I'm married," she told him, which, though true, was only part of the story. The last she'd heard from her husband, he'd dropped her a postcard from Portland, Oregon, on his way to Alaska.

"What's that got to do with your helping me out?"

"You always expect people to do things for you?"

He leaned forward. "I might just be looking for a business partner."

"And what kind of business would that be?"

"Any kind," he said. "Business is business." Then he gave her his card. It said, "Ray Hunsicker, Manager," followed by a telephone number. It didn't say manager of what.

He really did have a truck, which he'd named Dolly after his favorite brand of ice cream. The engine needed to be almost completely rebuilt. He'd traded a set of drums he bought at an auction for her. A Step-Van, ice-cream-truck white, she had been customized somewhere along the line, though crudely. Two bubble windows set into one side, a small platform bed in back. Christine got Dolly running for him, spending weekends out at his place, a little bungalow with a stream behind it where, after she'd cleaned up, they'd sit, drink beers together, and talk.

Ray seemed to know a little something about everything. He was an avid listener to the late-night call-in shows, particularly the financial ones. He believed in reincarnation, or said he did. He talked about zero coupon bonds, and the distinction between a single malt and a blend. He could play the whole guitar part to "In Memory of Elizabeth Reed," up until the solos kicked in, at which point he'd lean back, close his eyes, and just appreciate the genius of it. It had been Ray's idea to trailer down a load of Christmas trees and sell them on the streets of Manhattan, and she had to admit, it had worked out pretty well. They'd even sold the trailer at a profit. But it was possible to get drunk on your own success, and that was what Ray had fallen victim to. He just didn't have both feet on the ground.

She was worried. The days between Christmas and New Year's always made her feel unsettled anyway, and last night she'd had trouble sleeping — she'd kept jolting awake to frightening images. Ray knifed by a gang of gold-toothed black men, the truck set afire with them still in it. Ray lay beside her sleeping peacefully, bundled in his sleeping bag, unconcerned. She needed to pee, but not badly enough to get up. She stayed next to him, listening to the traffic and disembodied voices that passed by, her legs crossed, nose running with the cold, and waited for morning. They were in over their heads here. Now, the appearance of the dwarf only confirmed her suspicion that they had entered a grotesque land from which they would be lucky to return.

Two-nineteen was not the address K.C. had given them, it was the house next door, and it was by far the nicer of the two brownstones, with stained-glass windows over the door and a real gas lantern out in front. Both houses had appeared to be empty, but since it was between Christmas and New Year's, Ray pointed out, folks might be on vacation. "We'll just hang around and wait a while," he'd said.

For most of the afternoon she watched the dwarf and his companion moving in. The dwarf sat on the steps, giving directions in a shrill, irritated voice, smacking his small aluminum crutch against the metal railing for emphasis. He wore a parka with the hood up, so it was hard to see his face. They had a moving van, a rental with an enormous cowboy painted onto the side. It was a lot of work for one person. The black man, in sweatshirt and torn blue jeans, heaved chairs over his head, wrestled tables sideways, hoisted boxes in front of him. He paid little attention to the shouting of the dwarf.

One of the last things to go into the house was a guitar case. She kicked Ray to join her at the window. A Yamaha DX7 synthesizer followed, then a big cardboard box. "Home recording studio," Ray said. "The little guy's got money. That was a pretty decent guitar too, from the look of the case."

She looked at him for any sign of recognition as to what he'd said, since it was his ignorance on the subject of guitars that had brought them here in the first place. But he had his eyes to the window.

"Honey," she whispered. "Let's get out of here. We'll take the things to New Orleans and sell them there. We were dumb enough to buy them — someone else will be, too."

He sat back down and fumbled for a cigarette. "Nope," he said. "We wait for K.C."

"You know what he'll say. You didn't get cheated. You paid the money, you got the merchandise." She waved to the back of the van where the black cases lay stacked. "If we're going south, let's just go. We'll sell them, I know we will." She realized with a certain amount of disgust that she was pleading with him.

He said, "Trust me, I know what I'm doing."

"Ray," she said. "At least let's go back to the motel for the night. I need a shower, and you're no treat to be around either." Christmas night, after giving away the last of the trees, they'd driven through the Lincoln tunnel to New Jersey and stayed at an overpriced motel with porno movies available on cable. It wasn't great, but at least they'd had their own bathroom. Every time Christine went into the McDonalds they'd discovered on Nostrand Avenue, she felt like a criminal.

"I just want to square things, that's all. Then we hit the road."

"Square things? He'll probably put a bullet hole right through that tiny brain of yours. He'll probably make you eat those guitars one string at a time." She shook her head. "You are one stubborn sonofabitch," she said. "I'm sorry I came."

He turned and looked at her coldly. "Go on then. No one's keeping you. Forget Mardi Gras, forget the whole damn thing. Take a bus back home and get done with it. Just so's I don't have to live with your whining." He turned back to the window.

"You bastard," she said. "Give me my money."

· "What money?"

"Half of whatever's left. I worked for it."

He looked at her sullenly, then took out his wallet. She lifted it from his hand. "Two hundred and eighty," she said, counting. "I should take all of it." Stuffing half the bills into her jeans, she thrust the rest back at him, zipped up her coat, and slammed out of the truck.

The late afternoon sun had dropped behind the rooftops and the wind was bitter. She looked left, then right, trying to choose a direction. They were equally unappealing. In the distance a huge cigarette advertisement on the side of an elevated station hung across the street, green and blue, telling her to "Taste the Difference." Somewhere nearby a boom-box was cranked too high, its pounding bass a tired, steady raspberry. Out of the corner of her eye, she noticed an object lying on the steps of two-nineteen, a small alarm clock. It must have fallen from one of the boxes. She let herself in the gate, picked it up, paused for a moment, then went up and rang the bell. The black man answered the door.

She held out the clock. "It was on your steps."

He eyed it suspiciously, then took it from her and said, "Thank you."

From behind him a voice shouted, wanting to know who was there. It was a funny voice, Christine thought—reedy and childish.

"Just a neighbor," he called over his shoulder.

"Tell them to come in," said the voice. "It's all right, come in."

"Come in?" offered the black man.

"Well," said Christine, "for a little while." As she entered the house, she imagined Ray watching her every move from the freezing cargo area of the truck. With amazement, she hoped.

"I'll get Louis," said the man, leaving her alone in the living room, which was strewn with boxes waiting to be unpacked. The sofa was clear though, and a television had been set up. She sat down, unzipped her coat, blew on her hands to warm them, and wondered what next. A few moments later, Louis appeared, cradled in the big man's arms. He stuck out a hand and Christine shook it. It was surprisingly strong, and though small, seemed to expand in an attempt to enclose her own.

"Merry Christmas," he said. "Louis Martucci — producer and musician."

"Christine," she said. "From the neighborhood."

"A pretty name," he said. "You've met Dewayne. Excuse the mess — we just came from London. It's going to take a while to settle in. Dewayne, what about some wine? There's Beaujolais in the kitchen." He winked at her as Dewayne set him down on the floor. "We Italians love red wine," he said. "You're not Italian are you?"

She said she was sorry, but she wasn't. There followed a short, awkward silence during which she tried not to stare at him. He was so small.

"London?" she said, finally. "Why would you want to move here from London?"

Louis grinned and heaved himself a few inches forward on the floor, then tucked his legs together in front of him. "We weren't living there — it was a promotional tour. I make rap records."

"Really?" said Christine. Louis had an air of absolute self-confidence, and it made her tend to disbelieve him. Her image of people who made rap records involved sweat suits, high-top sneakers, sunglasses, and lots of jewelry.

Dewayne returned with two glasses of wine, handed her one and placed the other next to Louis.

"Maybe you've heard of us," said Louis. "Daddy D. and Short Time?"

"Which is which?"

"We're it. Both of us," said Dewayne.

Louis started to laugh. "A little joke we have," he said. "How do you like my house? Dewayne found it — he grew up around here. I was living with my parents, but we had some problems. Before we went to London I put my things in storage."

In spite of herself, she was staring at him, trying to judge his age, which might have been anywhere between twenty and forty. He'd already lost most of his hair, and his pronounced stomach made him look pregnant.

"I'm twenty-six," he said, guessing her thoughts. "But I started balding when I was fifteen."

"They say bald men are sexier." She was embarrassed as soon as she said it, but Louis was pleased. He rolled backward, laughing. He looked and sounded like a mechanical toy, she thought.

"Hey," he said, as he sat back up, "I like you—you're funny. I think we're going to be friends. More wine?"

"I don't know. I should probably be getting on."

Louis made a mock-angry face. "I'll be very insulted," he said. "I'm used to getting my way."

She sipped at her glass and considered. "All right, I guess I could stay a little while."

"Hooray," said Louis, spilling some from his own glass.

Dewayne touched him on the shoulder. "Bath."

"It's ready?" Louis asked.

"Just the way you like it."

"How about my rubber ducky?" He winked broadly at Christine, who smiled back at him. "Please, stay around for a while, at least until I'm out of the tub. We can talk some more."

She nodded and lifted her glass in salute as Dewayne hoisted Louis under the arms and carried him out of the room.

Christine put her feet up on the sofa and listened. From upstairs came the sound of rhythmic music playing quite loud, probably for her benefit. He was sitting in his tub, but his attention was all focused down here, with her. She lit a cigarette and thought about whether it would be rude to ask to use the bath herself.

Dewayne came back to pour her more wine. Then he just stood, watching her. She began to feel nervous.

"So," she said. "London."

"That's right," said Dewayne, his voice surprisingly soft. "But it wasn't that much of a vacation. Louis broke his leg and his hip as well. Been three weeks in the hospital."

"I'm sorry," she said. "What happened?"

"Nothing. He did it in his sleep. It happens fairly often. He has very fragile bones—no calcium in them. They never grew."

"So, it's really true? About the records and all?"

He looked at her curiously, as if judging her weight. "What makes you think it isn't?"

"Oh, I didn't say that. I'm just impressed, that's all. How did you two end up together?" Dewayne's large size was a little frightening. His hands looked like they'd been cast out of steel, and she was amazed every time he moved them.

"I answered an ad." He stood up and stretched his arms high over his head. "I'm going to check on Louis," he said. "Make yourself at home."

She went to the window and looked out at where the truck stood, silent and sad. The plan, pre-K.C., had been to use the tree money for New Orleans, taking time to see some of the country along the way. And after that just keep on going, maybe all the way up to the Northwest — Seattle or even Vancouver. The names had a misty, surreal quality for her — she imagined herself hiking at ten thousand feet, looking up at snowfields, across at even higher peaks. Her favorite reading material for the past year had been camping supply catalogues. She'd given her apartment key to her friend Claudia, who wanted it anyway, since her own marriage was looking more dubious by the day. There was no need for Christine to return, really. When they'd left she'd felt as if she and Ray were in one of those adventure movies, holding hands and leaping off a cliff together. She had no doubt that they'd land right in the middle of a big pile of feathers, or something equally astonishing.

The astonishment came from other quarters however. Standing on the streets of Manhattan freezing their toes off, surrounded by their own little conifer forest, Ray had let slip something about Nashville. It seemed he had a daughter there, not to mention an ex-wife. He'd never said anything before. Christine was furious.

"You dragged me on this expedition so you could go see your family for the holidays?"

"Of course not," he'd said. "Don't be stupid. I just want to stop in and say hi, that's all. It's on the way, more or less."

"I don't believe this."

He kicked at one of the trees. "OK, forget it, we won't go. It's just that it's Christmastime and it's been a while. If I'd known you'd get this upset I would never have said anything." With the thumb of his glove he wiped at his nose. "Jesus, if it's going to be this cold, the least it could do is snow."

She decided maybe she was being unreasonable after all. Sometimes you had to make compromises. That was how people got along.

"No, let's go," she told him. "I love kids."

He shook his head in disgust, as if the weather had reneged on some personal contract with him. "I mean, what's Christmas without the damn snow?"

Turning away from the window, she sat again on the sofa. What she resented about the whole thing was that the terms were no longer equal. She could even forgive him his stupidity about K.C. and the guitars. But Ray had a destination — Nashville, his daughter, his ex-wife. He hadn't cut totally loose the way she had, and it seemed unfair. It wasn't their trip anymore, it was his. Christine felt that now, in a sense, she was just along for the ride.

Dewayne brought Louis back out, this time dressed in a maroon sweat suit, the front unzipped to reveal a white muscle T-shirt. Everything was so tiny — children's clothes. He was clutching a bottle in his hands.

"Let's party," he said.

A pizza was delivered twenty minutes later by a man with dreadlocks, wearing two winter coats, one on top of the other, whom Dewayne seemed to know, since they talked for a while in the hall. When he left, the three of them ate in front of the TV. Louis kept up a steady stream of conversation, mostly about himself, and Christine found that if she just faced him and nodded her head occasionally, she wasn't required to do much at all in terms of holding up her end. She was dead tired. Dewayne was continually on the move, bringing things when Louis requested them, lifting boxes and carrying them off to other parts of the house.

Louis explained that he'd been making tapes since he was fifteen, but he'd only just sold his first record, to an independent label in England. The single was called "Chillin'," and already the BBC was giving it airplay.

"If you're not chillin', you're illin'," said Louis, grinning. "We did all the tracks in my parents' basement in Queens — synthesizers, electronic drums, everything. Dewayne did the words."

"Impressive," said Christine.

"I am a very gifted composer," Louis said. "And completely self-taught. I never played baseball—I sat in my basement making music. I can play classical, jazz, rock and roll—anything. But rap—that's where the energy is. Those people in London thought I was going to be black. Man, did we surprise them—they didn't even want to believe it. Like in the *Wizard of Oz*, you know? Pay no attention to that little man behind the curtain." He began a laugh that transformed into a violent chest cough. When he was through he wiped his eyes.

Dewayne put down the box he was lifting and stared at Louis.

"Dig it," said Louis. "Attitude is everything—that's one thing I've learned." His face was flushed with alcohol. He waved his glass. "More wine."

Dewayne shook his head. "That's it. You finished all three bottles.

"Then call the liquor store and have some sent."

"No phone yet, remember?"

"Well, maybe you ought to go for a walk," said Louis, his voice suddenly unpleasant.

The two of them eyed each other in silence for a moment.

"Do you think," Christine asked, "I could use your shower?"

Louis gave her an odd look.

"Mine's broken."

———

In the bathroom she stripped off her clothes and hung them from the inside knob. There was a bar of soap and a bottle of special shampoo for thinning hair already standing on the edge of the tub. She set the water temperature, stepped in, and pulled the curtain.

Under the hot spray she allowed herself to relax. Rather than trying to think, she let her various problems drift just beyond her reach—like floating toys in a swimming pool, if she made a move for them, they only edged farther away. Ray, the guitars, the strange company she now found herself in, it all seemed less important. Soaping herself, she realized that her hands no longer showed any trace of grease. Also, she was struck by how, around her knees and wrists, lines had formed that seemed particularly noticeable. She put her hands to her rear and decided for the hundredth time that it felt too soft. All her life she'd had a strong body, lean and hard. Somewhere along the way, when she wasn't paying attention, it had become womanly. She hated the word, but there it was. Things changed, whether you liked it or not.

For a moment, she had the sensation that she was being watched, though the plastic curtain made it hard to tell for sure. She tried to whistle, but found it impossible with all the water, so instead hummed loudly. It seemed the air temperature had dropped. When she finished up and stepped out to dry, she saw that the door was open, just a crack. She was sure she'd closed it.

When she returned to the living room, she found Louis seated in a chair with his back to her. Dewayne was at the window, looking out.

"Still there," he said.

"Damn," said Louis.

"What's still there?" she asked.

Louis turned around. "Our neighbor has returned," he said, his voice almost accusing. "Somebody parked a truck outside with out-of-state plates. Dewayne says it's drugs. I say it's stolen. What do you think?" He glared at her for a moment, then began to cough again, a fit that lasted a full thirty seconds. "I need my medicine," he said at last, red-faced.

Dewayne made to pick him up, but Louis shook him off with a violent gesture and, retrieving his crutches, hobbled uncertainly out of the room.

There was a brief, awkward silence in his wake. Christine thought she ought to explain. "Actually," she said, "that's my truck. Well, my friend's."

"I know," Dewayne said.

"You do?"

"I saw you both earlier. You and the man. I'm not blind. But I don't know what you want to come park yourselves in this part of town for."

"We were looking for a man who cheated us out of some money. Jamaican guy with gold teeth? He said his name was K.C." She knew it was dumb to think that Dewayne might know him. Still, it was worth a try. She felt suddenly reconnected to Ray, freezing his bones in the back of the truck, feeling twice betrayed, first by K.C., now by her.

Dewayne laughed. "K.C.? Sure, I know K.C. Used to live next door a couple of years ago. Just got out of jail, I think. Forget about your money."

"We thought maybe if we talked to him."

"Darling, I don't know what department store you think you went to."

From the other room, Louis was shouting something, his tone that of a spoiled child throwing a tantrum. She thought again of the open bathroom door, and felt suddenly angry.

"Why do you put up with him?" she asked. "I wouldn't."

Dewayne stuck his hands in his pockets. "The man's body is wearing out at the rate of about five years for every one of yours or mine. A thing like that tends to make you a little unpleasant." He turned and looked out the window, toward the truck. "Parents don't know where he is, just that he went to London and now he's back. They'll be looking for him, if they aren't already."

"Short Time," she said, embarrassed. "I get it."

"Funny, right? It was his idea."

"You still didn't say why you stay with him."

"He pays me."

She tried to think of something to say to this that wouldn't sound insensitive. "At least his song is doing well," she said. "That's something."

"There's no song. I mean, there's a lot of tape, you know. But the rest of it — that stuff about the BBC — it's all in Louis's head. Make-believe."

"You went all the way to London for an imaginary meeting?"

"Why not? It's Louis's money. He's not crazy — he just needs to be humored. Nothing unusual about that — we could all use a little humoring. That's what he pays me for."

"Oh." She was convinced it was more complicated. She had the idea that Dewayne needed Louis, too, in some way beyond a simple paycheck.

"He thinks you may be some kind of spy."

"Spy?"

"From his parents. I told you, they don't know where he is, and they do have a lot of money."

Outside, Ray had turned on the truck's lights. A cough of white smoke spat from the exhaust.

"Your friend is getting tired of waiting."

Christine didn't like being pushed, but at the same time she was afraid to stay. If Ray left, that was it. Nothing awaited her back home except plugs and timing belts and gaskets and valves. Even more, she worried for Ray, whose belief in the future was matched only by his inability to get along at all in the present. He was going to need her.

"Tell Louis good-bye for me," she said, zipping up her coat. Outside, the red taillights amidst all the smoke made the truck look like a waiting dragon.

Something small and hard struck her in the leg. Then another object smacked into the door beside her. Louis had come back into the room, a bag of apples clutched in his teeth. He'd set down his crutches and was throwing the fruit at her.

"Get out!" he shouted. "This is my house!"

She started toward him. Another apple caught her in the thigh. Her impulse was to simply pick him up and give him a spanking. But then she thought of what Dewayne had said, and it made her stop. He was too delicate — inside his round, doughy outsides, he was a piece of fine, thin crystal. She might kill him.

Dewayne moved to block the path between her and Louis with his body, but not before another apple came winging at her face. She caught this one one-handed, the movement so automatic it surprised even her. With a certain satisfaction, she stuck it in her pocket, turned, and walked out the door. As she left, she heard Dewayne's voice speaking to Louis in low, calming tones.

———

At the motel where they stopped that night, Ray continued to keep quiet, just as he had most of the trip since Christine had hopped up next to him in the front of the truck. He was feeling foolish, she knew, and she took no pleasure in it. They shared a pint bottle of Jim Beam, mixing it with Pepsi from the machine outside their room, each of them seated cross-legged on the enormous double bed. They smoked a bunch of cigarettes. K.C.'s karma would catch up with him in the end, Ray said finally. In his next life he'd be a talking clown at a Jack in the Box drive-thru.

Later, he wanted to watch television, an HBO movie about gangsters, with seminudity and stupid dialogue. She slid under the covers, pretending to fall asleep. It was Ray who fell asleep first though—his tall, skinny frame looking deflated and awkward stretched across the flowered bedspread. Christine took his shoes off and put the covers over him. Then she pulled on her jeans, slipped into her jacket, and stepped outside. Dolly stood quietly waiting by their door, and though Christine had grown to hate the truck over the past week, there now seemed something almost friendly about it.

She looked up. Most of the sky was covered by a dull, milky haze, but there was one area that still remained clear, a round tear in the fabric like a dark tunnel outward. It amazed her to think that while all these planets, including her own, were hurtling around the galaxy, she could still stand here with both feet planted firmly on the ground. Stability, she decided, was always an illusion to some extent. The thing was not to look backward, but to confront the darkness head on, and not blink. Tomorrow, they'd head on toward Nashville. At least it was likely to be warmer there, and she supposed one ex-wife wasn't all that big a deal. Something touched her lightly through the torn knee of her jeans and she jumped, thinking it felt like a small finger, but then realized. It had only begun to snow.

# BLUESTOWN

When I was fifteen, my father showed up at our high school and stood outside the door of Mr. Margin's history class wearing his leather jacket, waving a pink piece of paper. It was a September afternoon, sunny but not too hot, the sky bright blue. I had been alternately staring out the window and making eyes at Lucy Westbrook who sat opposite me, and had probably the nicest body in the whole school. Mr. Margin stopped lecturing (the subject was, I think, slavery) and went to the door, then gestured for me to step out into the hall with him.

"You're excused Spencer," he said. "It seems you've forgotten something."

I didn't know what he was talking about, but the prospect of getting out of that stuffy classroom was an unexpected gift.

"Your doctor's appointment, Spence," said my dad, pointing to his watch. "We're late already." He had this concerned, fatherly expression on his face, and looked at Mr. Margin in commiseration. "I knew he'd forget. He's known about this for weeks."

"It's my experience," said Mr. Margin, "that given half a chance, these kids will forget anything. Get a move on Spencer — read the next chapter for tomorrow's class." He gave me an affectionate smack on the shoulder.

"Kids," said my dad to him, then led me down the hall. When we got to the front entrance, he looked both ways, then began to run. He took off across the front lawn, past a group of kids sharing a joint, nearly tripping over a girl who was stretched out in the sun. I ran after him, thinking that this time he had finally, truly lost it. When I caught up with him at his car, a '67 Buick station wagon with a wired-on front bumper, I could see the back was loaded with equipment — all his guitars, an amplifier, and a suitcase. I got in the passenger side as he started up the engine.

"What's going on?" I asked when I'd caught my breath.

He slipped on a pair of aviator sunglasses. "It's way too nice a day to hang out in school," he said.

He loved to break rules — it was one of the things I liked best about him. It was also part of the reason he'd been banished, several years before, from the small ranch house where my mother and I still lived along with Hal, her new husband. My dad, a few gray traces just beginning to appear in the hair that fell over his ears, now inhabited a small apartment downtown, over Angelo's Pizza and Calzone. I still saw a lot of him, more than my mother would have liked. He was only supposed to get me one day a week, but I'd go over to his place after school and hang around listening to albums, or playing cards. Since his work, when he had any, was at night, he was home afternoons. He liked to talk about the old days, when rock and roll was still counterculture and not just something else to show on TV. We'd sit on his secondhand sofa bed, albums and cassette tapes strewn over the floor, the smell of pizza wafting up through the floorboards, and he'd tell me how he was never really cut out to be a family man. Possessions and responsibilities made him nervous, even things like his stereo and television. Even so, whenever he did get some money, he'd spend it on a new toy—a phase-shifter or a compressor, or maybe a graphic EQ—and together we'd spend hours fooling with the knobs and buttons.

He played me albums, everything from Robert Johnson and Lightnin' Hopkins to Jimi Hendrix and Duane Allman. Guitar, he said, was the only instrument on which you could really play the blues. I was familiar with all sorts of obscure, Chicago-based players, most of them named Milton or Melvin. I fully believed I knew what it meant to have the blues. In school I covered my notebooks with drawings of guitars and amps. My prize possession was a Muddy Waters T-shirt he brought me back from New York once, and which I wore so often my mother had to swipe it from my room just to get it washed. With my friends I smoked cigarettes and kept my hands plunged deep into my pockets, nodding in time to an imaginary beat. What I liked above all things was the tortured sound of a guitar string, bent almost to the point of breaking.

I asked about all the equipment, and he explained that he had an audition in Montreal for a gig with a new band that had backing, a recording contract—everything but the right guitarist. This seemed major—there was an intensity on his face that I couldn't remember seeing. When I asked him how they happened to come up with *his* name, he just smiled and said "a friend of a friend." My dad had a lot of friends.

He made a living as a guitarist, more or less. It always seemed he was on the verge of success when something would happen. My mother said he brought it on himself, but as far as I could see, he just ran into a lot of bad luck. For a while he'd pinned his hopes on a local woman named Maddie Kelso—an emaciated redhead with an enormous, whiskey-steeped voice. He worked with her for about a year, but she got born again and moved to Wisconsin. Another time he left his car unlocked and all his instruments were stolen, so for months he had to borrow equipment. But he stayed optimistic, full of plans, and even my mom, on the uncomfortable occasion when she would run into him at the supermarket or the drugstore, found it hard to be angry with him. She didn't like us spending time together and said he was a bad role model, but he could always do something dumb, like wiggle his eyebrows at her, or juggle a couple of avocados, and at least get a laugh.

We went to the Dairy Queen and had black-and-white milk shakes. It was where the greasers hung out, and the parking lot was full of them: slicked-back hair, big combs sticking out of the back pockets of their polyester pants. They leaned against jacked-up cars, smoked cigarettes, ignored the girlfriends who lounged next to them, all hair spray and lip gloss, car radios blaring. With his leather jacket, worn-out jeans, and shades, my dad was easily the coolest-looking person there. I liked the way we could just hang out together on the hood of the Buick, feeling the hot metal under our legs, sipping a cold shake.

"Jimi," he said. It was something we'd done since I was little — calling each other by the names of dead guitarists. I got to be Jimi, and he was Duane, after Duane Allman, who was definitely the closest thing to a hero in his life. Nobody'd ever played slide like Duane, or ever would.

"They sent me expense money," he said.

"Great," I said. "That means they're serious."

He shrugged. "I guess. The way I see it, if I drive up, it costs me next to nothing and I pocket the difference. What do you say? Feel like a road trip?"

I could think of nothing I felt like more. An image of the two of us cruising north through New England flashed through my mind like the trailer for a sixties road movie. But, I pointed out, my mother was going to be a problem.

He lowered his voice. "We won't tell her — we'll just leave a note saying you're with me, and when we get back, I'll take all the heat."

A note from him wasn't going to get me out of anything, but I wanted to go, so I convinced myself it was a workable plan. After all, it would just be a couple of days.

"It feels a little like running away from home," I said, enjoying the idea. A friend of mine, Nicky Dormer, had run away from home for four days the year before, and afterward he'd seemed to me years older.

"Jimi, my man," he answered, massaging my shoulders. "It is impossible to run away from home with your own father."

My mom was still at work. We drove by the house and I ran upstairs to get a toothbrush while he stood in the kitchen penciling a quick note in his own, peculiarly recognizable handwriting—an angular sort of chicken scratch. When I came back down he was still laboring over it. It was odd seeing him there, back in the house for the first time in years. He looked uncomfortable, out of place. I looked at what he wrote, but it wasn't until we were in the car and heading out of town that I asked him about it.

"Hey, Duane," I said, "How come you put down that we were going to Virginia?"

"Just a precaution," he said. "In case she decides to call the cops, it'll buy us some time."

———

As soon as we were on the road, he slipped in a cassette of the Allman Brothers doing "Statesboro Blues," and I kicked my feet up on the dashboard. The music almost seemed to be powering the car. I'd seen pictures from back when I was only about three or four, when my dad practically *was* Duane Allman. He wore his hair all the way down his back and had the same muttonchop side-burns. The day after Duane died on his motorcycle, my dad managed to get into an accident on his. He broke a leg and an arm, but he also got an out-of-court settlement that was enough to buy our house, as well as a good PA system and a couple of guitars. He was twenty-five years old, a high school graduate with a wife, a kid, and his own place. Things started to happen. Weird people would come over in the middle of the night to hang out, and in the morning there'd be spilled beer and cigarette burns in the carpet. My mom and he would fight, then he'd disappear for a couple of days at a time. Afterward he'd always try to make up for it by doing something real normal, like mowing the lawn, or taking the three of us out to the movies.

Finally, she just told him to move. I was nine. "Buddy," he said to me, "I'm not going anywhere." He wrote his new phone number on the inside of a book of matches and put it in my hand.

_____

We stopped for gas at a turnpike service station and he pulled out his wallet. It was stuffed with bills, more money than I'd ever seen him with at one time. He removed a ten and gave it to me. "Candy bars," he said, solemnly.

I got change and pushed quarters into the machine until I had extracted four Snickers, our favorite. Then, on impulse, I also bought a pair of cheap amber-tinted sunglasses that were aviators like his. They were small on me and rode high on the bridge of my nose. They cost six dollars and were probably worth about forty-nine cents, but I bought them anyway. When I got back to the car he lifted them off and bent the flimsy frame across the middle, just slightly, then put them back on me.

"That's it," he said. "Now you're cooking."

_____

As we drove, we talked about Canada. Neither of us had ever been, so we made a list of things it was famous for.

"Canadian bacon," I offered.

"Salmon," he said.

"The Expos."

"Draft dodgers."

"Niagara Falls."

"That's in America."

"Only part of it. The other part is Canadian."

He looked over at me. "Who figured that out?"

"It makes sense. It's a natural divider. That's how they always divide up countries. States too." When he didn't say anything, I fell silent for a little while, thinking about how things divided. How did they know exactly where Canada stopped and America began? It was all just water — there couldn't be any clear line like on a map. I thought about me and my dad — I was halfway to thirty, and he was halfway to seventy. I always had an idea that when I turned eighteen I would experience some obvious transformation into adulthood, but now that I was getting closer, I wondered. The twenty years that separated me from my dad suddenly seemed like nothing at all, if you looked at the whole picture.

———

We crossed the Vermont border around sunset and stopped for burgers at a place with two enormous trucks parked outside. It was a classic roadside diner, but somehow not quite real — everything in it was brand-new, though styled to look mid-fifties. It was someone's idea of what a diner should have looked like — lots of chrome and mirrors and a big, colorful jukebox. I put a quarter in and selected two songs.

"If they like you, does that mean you'll have to move to Canada?" I asked, coming back to the table.

"Could be," he said. "I don't know. It all depends."

I pictured his apartment over the pizzeria and tried to imagine someone else living there, but it just didn't seem a real possibility. "I'd miss you," I said. "Where would I hang out?"

He tapped the tabletop with his fork. "Well, let's not count our chickens. They may not want me at all. I'm getting kind of old for this line of work."

"How can you say that? Look at the Stones. Look at . . . " I tried to think of someone else. "B. B. King. He's still going, and he must be about sixty."

He yawned. His eyes were red from all the driving, and he looked tired. "I don't know," he said. "The way I see it, this may be my last shot. If it isn't happening, I may just try to get into something respectable."

"Like Hal?" Hal was in insurance, and we had a fair amount of fun at his expense. Both of us thought insurance was about the most boring thing you could possibly do, and that by marrying Hal my mother had not so much found a mate as taken out a policy. Actually though, I kind of liked him. He never tried to be my father, he was just Hal. He left me alone when I didn't want to be bothered, and he was an incredible cook.

"Exactly. How do you think I'd look in a suit and tie?" He

picked up his glasses and pointed them at me, businesslike. "Let's talk coverage," he said in his best salesman's voice. "You tell me you play in a band? Fine. Say one day you get up there on stage, put a hand on your guitar, the other on the microphone. And let's just say that system isn't properly grounded. In one blue flash you get zapped right into the next state. What about your wife? Your kids? Who takes care of them? The musicians' union? You say you're not in the union? Well, I have a little policy designed just for you. We call it the Guitar Player's Friend—it provides all-purpose coverage for you and your loved ones, and it's issued by the Chuck Berry Mutual Accident and Life Insurance Company, a name you've known and trusted for years. Believe me, you won't want to plug in without it."

The waitress interrupted him with our food. I waved a french fry. "Brilliant," I said. "You could be rich."

"Yeah, maybe," he said modestly. "I'd like to think I'll be able to leave you something someday." He sipped his coffee. "If you had all the money you could ever want, what would you do?"

I chewed and thought. "I don't know, I guess I'd buy about ten guitars, a small recording studio, and some video equipment."

He nodded. "And live where?"

"Hawaii maybe. The Swiss Alps."

"Good choices," he said. "A little romantic, but you're supposed to be romantic at fifteen."

"So? What would you do?" I asked.

"I believe," he said, "I'd do exactly what I'm doing right now."

———

He was tired and didn't feel like driving much more, so we started looking around for a place to stay. Since we were in Vermont, he said, we ought to find one of those quaint country inns where you slept under thick goose down comforters and they served you up a big New England style breakfast in the morning. We must have spent an hour driving around trying to find one. Eventually we settled on a motor court called Traveller's Rest, with a blinking neon sign of a sheep jumping over the name. The parking lot was empty, and my dad kept shaking his head over the fact that the one time he actually wanted to spend some money he couldn't find a way to do it, but I was happy. This was much more the kind of place I'd imagined crashing for the night, and as for the rest of that stuff, it wasn't really cold enough for a down comforter, and I was never much on breakfasts.

Our room was hooked up with cable television, and I immediately found an old movie that looked good, a British vampire flick with lots of gore and women nearly tumbling out of their bodices. My dad spent ten minutes going back and forth to the car bringing in all his guitars. It seemed a little odd to me that he'd bothered to take every single one of them along, but I didn't say anything. This was a very big audition for him, and I figured he needed the extra confidence. He took a pint bottle of Chivas Regal out of his bag, went into the bathroom, and returned with two tissue-wrapped glasses. I'd never had Chivas, but I remembered reading on an album cover that it was John Lee Hooker's favorite drink. I squinched over to make room for him on the bed, then took the glass he handed me. He turned the sound on the television down.

"Your mother called me last week," he said, after a moment. "Says you're messing up in school."

"That's not true," I told him. "Just one class. I'm getting B's in everything else. Anyhow, why should she call you?"

"She wants us to stop hanging around together so much, at least till your grades pick up."

We almost never talked about school, except in the most general way, and having him speak to me like this — father to son, when we were now hundreds of miles from home — seemed a kind of betrayal.

"That's stupid," I said.

He nodded.

"I hope that's what you told her."

"I didn't tell her anything," he said. "I wanted to talk to you first."

I was suddenly angry at my mother for trying to interfere so blatantly with my life, and behind my back, too. I wasn't a kid anymore. I had been thinking about calling her, just to let her know I was all right, but now I felt like letting her stew a little.

"You know," he said, lying back on the bed and crossing his legs, "she's probably right. I'm thirty-five, still kicking around the same town I grew up in, still trying to land a steady gig. Being with me isn't going to help you become CEO of General Motors."

"Come on," I said. "You're my dad." I sipped at my drink, which made my eyes water.

"OK," he said, studying me. "I just wanted to make sure."

A question occurred that I was almost afraid to ask. "Could she do something? Something legal I mean?"

"I don't know," he said. "It's a possibility." He got up and went into the bathroom to pee.

I made a promise to myself that regardless of what happened, things would continue on between us the way they always had. It was hard to imagine my mother actually doing something so drastic, but taking off without her permission had already given me a sense of power. Things could be any way I wanted them to be, I thought. What were they going to do, put me under armed guard?

"How long do you think we'll stay in Montreal?" I asked when he came back.

He looked through the blinds out at the parking lot. "Not long. A couple of days, tops." Then he slapped a hand down on my leg. "What do you say we head out and see if there's any nightlife around here?"

I jumped up and turned off the set.

———

We drove around until we found a little roadside place called Mother's that had pickup trucks parked outside and a flashing red Miller sign in the window. There were maybe twenty-five people inside, not counting the band — five bored-looking guys in checked shirts playing sleepy country tunes. The guitar player didn't look much older than me, in spite of an attempted mustache. When we walked in I immediately sensed hostility, but I just followed my dad. He walked to the bar, took a seat, ordered us drinks, and helped himself to a handful of peanuts from a bowl they had out. I reached in and grabbed a couple too. The bartender pursed his lips and considered me for a moment, then shrugged and uncapped us two longneck bottles of Bud.

"Never order anything fancy in a strange bar," said my dad, tipping back his bottle. "The first thing people notice about you in a place like this is what you're drinking."

I nodded. We sat for a while, just swigging beer. Then I got up to go to the bathroom, and when I got back he was in a conversation with a fat guy he introduced as Al. Al worked as a mechanic, he said. He had huge, grease-blackened hands.

"This your kid?" asked Al.

My dad smiled proudly and I stood there feeling like a prize hog. I wished I were still back in the motel room watching television.

"I got a kid," said Al. I waited for him to say something else, but for Al, the statement was a complete thought, and he just turned and faced the bar.

The band shuddered to a halt and went on break, and my dad ordered a round of shots for them, digging into his stuffed wallet and tossing a twenty onto the bar. Then he left me and Al sitting together, went over and got talking to the guitarist and bass player. I thought about all the bars in our town where he'd played. He was always in trouble with the club owners for showing up late, or mixing up dates, but he could smooth-talk them and manage to get hired again regardless. His ability in this respect was legendary. One time he got himself booked into two different places with different bands on the same night, and rather than cancel, did half of one gig, then drove to the other and finished up the night there, using me as an excuse. "You came down with a convenient case of the mumps," he explained the next day. "I could never have made it without you." For two days after that, I walked around faking a cough and trying to look weak, just in case someone should want to check out his story.

Al wasn't much of a talker, so I drank at my beer and tried to pretend that hanging around in a bar was the most natural thing in the world for me. I counted the bottles of liquor lined up next to the cash register.

"Jimi," said my dad, coming over and poking me in the side. "We're going to sit in next set. What do you say?"

I looked into his eyes to see if he was kidding. I played a little guitar, but not very well, and never in front of people. The prospect terrified me, and I could see he was serious. "You go ahead," I said. "I'll watch."

"Come on, we'll do some blues." He smiled encouragingly.

"I can't," I said. "Really."

"Sure you can," he told me.

I felt something close to panic, but at the same time it didn't seem that I had any choice. They had an extra guitar on stage for me, and the band's guitarist handed his over to my dad. When he did that he gave me a little smile that made the few dark hairs spread out on his upper lip. I took it as a sign of encouragement and plugged in. My dad called out "Red House," a Hendrix tune he knew I knew, and started playing. I tried to follow along, but after a few seconds I realized something was off.

My guitar was tuned a peculiar way. The chords I formed were one disaster after another. My dad kept giving me furious looks, as if I was deliberately screwing around. Everything I played came out wrong. He leaned over and shouted something to me that I could not hear above the music. I could see the band's guitarist leaning against the bar, laughing. I did the only thing I could think of — I stopped playing. Or rather, I pretended to play, damping the strings with my left hand so that no sound came out. My dad shook his head, turned away, and began to sing.

He played particularly well. Toward the end he picked up an empty Budweiser bottle and ran it along the strings for a slide, while I mimed along, numb, waiting for it to be over. We got hoots of approval and applause, but I barely heard them in my rush to get off.

The band's guitarist said something to me as he took the instrument out of my hands. I jumped down, ignoring the amusement in his eyes, and went and stood next to a shuffleboard table while my dad talked to some of the locals — bearded men in checked wool jackets who clapped him on the back and offered to buy him drinks. Finally he came over to me.

"Let's go," I said.

It was cold in the parking lot, the air smelling of pine, the muted sounds of the bar mixing with the swell and hush of the wind in the trees. My dad walked me to the car and unlocked it.

"It was in open tuning," he said, finally. "Set up for slide."

"Yeah?" I said. "How was I supposed to know that?"

"You know about open tuning. All you had to do was think."

"I *couldn't* think!" I practically shouted. "Nothing sounded right and I didn't know what to do!"

"So what?" he said. "You just quit? You can't let yourself get beat like that."

"I didn't."

"Well, what do you call it?" He was glaring at me, and I could see that he was really upset about this, more so even than I was.

"I didn't quit," I said quietly. "I stayed up there with you."

———

We drove in a silence that I was afraid to break; the longer it went on the more permanent it felt. He wouldn't look at me. He was speeding, too, I noticed, but I wasn't going to say anything. Then, about a mile from our motel we got pulled over by the cops.

As the officer shined his flashlight into our faces, I thought about the note we'd left. If my mother really had reported us to the police, this was probably it. I wondered what, if anything, they could do to him. I suspected he could get in a lot of trouble. Mostly though, I was worried he might not get to the audition, and that it would somehow be my fault. I sat frozen in anticipation, the cold night air flowing against my face from the open window, hoping as hard as I could for nothing bad to happen.

"Been doing a little drinking tonight?" asked the policeman as he examined my dad's license.

"Yes sir," he said. "Two beers. But I'm sober."

The cop pointed his flashlight in my face. "Who's that?"

"My son."

"Is that right?" He turned the light away from me and back at my dad. "Taking a little vacation are you?"

"You might say that."

"OK, out of the car."

I had to sit for ten minutes while they ran him through a series of tasks to determine whether he was drunk. It was hard to watch. He walked a straight line four times, and counted backward from fifty twice. All the while, another cop sat behind us, just a silhouette under the flashing blue light, speaking into his radio. They were checking on us. They didn't believe he was my father.

Finally, they wrote out a ticket and let us go. Just like that. This seemed incredible luck to me, and as soon as we were back under way, I let out a little whoop.

"Man," I said. "That was close."

But he still wasn't talking. In fact, he wouldn't even look at me. I wanted to tell him it didn't matter, to just forget it, but I couldn't. He didn't say anything at all until we got back to the motel. He put out a hand and tugged at the top of my head, then ran it down the back of my neck.

"You could use a haircut," he said.

———

When I woke the next morning, he was in the bathroom, shaving. I went and leaned against the door, watching him slide the razor carefully along the contours of his throat. He put a finger on his nose and pushed it comically to one side to get at his upper lip, turned and made a face at me. I liked seeing him shave. Getting my toothbrush, I fought him for sink space. When he pushed back, I pushed harder, then scooped water out of the sink and splashed him. He dropped the razor, picked up the can of shaving cream and advanced toward me, his face spotted with islands of foam. I ran, but he cornered me by the television and emptied half the can onto my head before I managed to wrestle it out of his hands. We stood there for a while, the two of us covered in shaving cream, laughing. Then he took the can from my hands, flipped it once in the air and went back into the bathroom.

We reloaded the car and checked out. He paid cash for the room and asked the guy at the desk where we could get a good breakfast. He recommended a place about three miles away that turned out to be one of those country-style inns we'd been hoping to find the night before, and had in fact driven right past. We were both starved, and my dad told me to order a dream breakfast — anything I thought I could possibly eat. I had four eggs, home fries, sausages, waffles, toast, orange juice, and coffee. He had steak and eggs with fried onions. The waitress looked a little hassled bringing out all that food — there was barely room for the plates — but we got a kick out of being so extravagant, and we tipped her heavily when we were through. After all, it wasn't our money.

We hit the road about eleven, windows open, tape deck turned up full. We sang along with some old Traffic and Santana, and I beat out rhythms by banging one hand on the glove compartment and the other against the roof of the car. It was a perfect day to be driving, and north seemed the only direction possible. The Buick's big engine hummed powerfully in front of us, and even the air tasted like Canada — cool and fresh and full of promise.

"Hey," I said to him. "What do you say after Montreal we just keep on going? We could set a record. First station wagon to reach the North Pole."

"Bad idea," he said, adjusting his glasses with his forefinger.

"Why?"

"Because. Too much competition. The North Pole is swarming with guitarists already."

I kept quiet.

He closed his eyes for a moment. "They've got this little town up there. It's jointly owned by all the major record companies."

"Not a very pleasant place to live," I said.

"That's the whole point, it's a miserable place to live." He reached over and turned the stereo down. "Bluestown," he said. "Most of the greats are up there, on salary, just biding their time. Muddy Waters, Jimi Hendrix, Duane Allman, Elmore James. All of them hanging out, drinking, jamming and trying to keep warm."

I forced a laugh, but I wondered. Sometimes he seemed to have no notion of how old I was. Or even that I was there at all. "So what you're saying is that they're actually still alive?"

"That's exactly what I'm saying. Where do you think they keep getting those 'newly discovered' tapes from? The blues wasn't selling, so they figured this would be a good way to stir up interest. And let me tell you something, a couple of years from now the world is going to be in for one hell of a surprise. Because they're coming back, all of them."

"Return of the Killer Guitarists," I said in my best coming-attractions voice. "When is this going to happen?"

He shrugged. "Who knows? When we're ready for them, I guess. When everyone has had enough of the crap they play on the radio."

"Bluestown." I flipped through the road atlas. "You know, it's not here on the map."

"It's there. Trust me. You just go to Chicago, then head due north."

"But," I pointed out, "the North Pole is due north of every-where, not just Chicago."

"Hey," he said. "Don't argue with your father."

———

I nodded off for a while, imagining a town built entirely of ice, with fur-bundled shapes walking up and down the streets carrying guitar cases. I kept thinking, How do I know these people are who they say they are if I can't see their faces? Then we got off the highway and I woke up. We were a little south of St. Johnsbury. My dad said he wanted to take a few minutes and look at a typical New England town. The place was called Denton, and it was truly quaint: tree-lined streets, big old houses with well-kept yards, two neat, white-steepled churches, only a couple of blocks apart. It was one of those picture postcards of a town, and I thought it probably didn't look any different now than it had fifty years ago. I couldn't imagine what people there did for a living, but everyone we saw looked reasonably well off. We drove up and down its few streets, looking at the houses, and just enjoying the simplicity of the place. In the center of town, he pulled over by the bus station and put the car in neutral.

"How about a couple of candy bars before we get going?" he said.

I was still stuffed from breakfast, and I couldn't imagine that he was actually hungry again, but I said sure and hopped out of the car. He stuck his hand out the window with a five dollar bill in it. I took the money and went inside.

It was a tiny bus station, just a window, a bench, and two vending machines. The guy at the window was out of singles, and I waited while he counted the whole five out in quarters, nickels and dimes. Then I bought two Snickers bars. With them in my hand, I stepped back out into the bright sunlight.

He was already gone. I could see the tailgate of the station wagon bouncing away from me down the street in the distance. I stood there watching him go, thinking that any moment now he would turn around and come back. It had to be a joke. But he kept going until the car disappeared over a crest.

I stared after him down the street. I was standing alone in the middle of a tiny Vermont town with two chocolate bars in my hand and no idea what to do next. Then I stuck my hand in my jacket pocket and felt the wad of money. He had slipped it there somehow without my noticing, and when I took it out I counted nearly seven hundred dollars, most of it in fifties and twenties. I sat down right where I was on the curb.

It took a little while to collect myself. I walked up and down the main street of Denton, Vermont, looking into shop windows, kicking at loose stones on the street. I opened one of the candy bars and took a bite, but dropped the rest of it in a trash can. I took out the roll of money again, fanned through it. This time, a small slip of yellow paper fell out from between two of the fifties. Picking it up, I saw that it was a withdrawal slip for just over nine hundred dollars from my father's bank, and on it in a teller's handwriting were the words Account Closed.

I stood for a while feeling the sun on my face, looking up at a solid blue sky that extended, unbroken, right up to the Canadian border and beyond. There was no audition. There had only been, for a brief while, an idea about the two of us starting over again someplace else, and maybe this time getting it right. I thought I understood what it felt like to look at your own future and see nothing but disappointment and failure stretching out like an endless series of clouds. The thing was, if he'd asked, I would have kept going. Taking all the change I had in my pockets, I began feeding the parking meters of downtown Denton, Vermont, pumping each one hard until it would take no more, then moving on to the next. After a while, when I ran out of coins, I stepped back into the dark little bus station and paid for a one-way ticket home.

*Previous Winners of the*